CHRIS PEASE

Under The Skin

Without the support of my parents, my partner Hannah, who constantly pushed me to keep writing and the expert eye of my proof reader Catherine, this book would never be what it has become today. Here's to step one of this wild journey. . .

Prologue

Doctor Yasmin King slid across the makeshift corridor and scrabbled for grip on the plastic sheeting as she attempted to move swiftly. It screamed again, but it sounded far enough away for her to be able to sit down - just for a moment.

Continuing, she reached the end of the corridor, swung herself over and leaned against the wall. She pulled her arm in front of her and glanced down at the deep cuts, blood trickling from them and pooling to her side, slowly covering her lower half. Her breathing became faster as panic set in. She slowly turned away from her arm, closing her eyes and trying to hold it together. Another scream filled the air, sounding like something was moving nearby again. Alarmed, Yasmin pushed herself awkwardly away from the wall, slipping in her own blood as she staggered down the corridor leaving behind a trail of bloodied boot prints. The walls were riddled with bullet holes and small nicks, reminders of the wild battles that had taken place in the hub. The wind howled through them, sounding like an out of tune instrument. The hub was now more of a morbid eyesore than the exciting research station she had settled into just a few weeks ago.

Yasmin patted her lab coat and found the device she still had safely stored in one of the deep pockets. Sighing with relief, she steadily made her way deeper into the hub, desperate in her mission to reach the command zone. She paused briefly before pushing through the blood splattered sheet that separated one area from another. Despite her apprehension, she stumbled and slid across the floor. She fell, landing awkwardly, she grunted in pain as her arm became pressed against her own body. Slowly, she pushed herself up as the power cut out once again.

"Shit no, come on!"

Yasmin glanced around and staggered across the floor. As the power returned, she froze as she found herself staring at the dead bodies of a group of her colleagues, their corpses spread out around the room. They were battered and torn both inside and out; their blood now mingling with the vile, green liquid which they had discovered in the debris field. Desperate to avoid it, Yasmin stumbled backwards. As she moved, the liquid seemed to slither towards her. In agony, she pulled herself up using the table that had once housed her research, sobbing as she moved out of her old working quarters. Glancing back at her dead colleagues and friends, she wondered how this whole situation was even possible.

Her stalker screamed again. Yasmin stopped as she put her arm through the plastic sheeting. She was a few steps away from the command hub's radio - just six, maybe seven, steps, perhaps a three second sprint to the console. She closed her eyes as her stalker hissed, the noise growing ever nearer as it stalked the corridor, pulling the material with it, tearing it apart like a knife. Yasmin could feel the icy air around her beginning to climb her back. She shivered as her body was cooled by the sudden change in temperature, her arms ached as her wounds reacted to the cold. Yasmin took a deep breath and dashed through the sheeting. Her stalker screamed again in response and she could hear it sprinting towards her with incredible speed.

Yasmin stepped over the bodies of the soldiers that had made it inside then ground to a halt at the communication station. She pushed an unfortunate soul from his chair, his lifeless body falling to the floor with a muffled thud. She pulled the headphones from the soldier's disfigured head. Putting them on, she could feel the dead man's blood drip from them into her black hair as she frantically tugged at the device in her pocket, retrieving it with relief. She pushed it into the machine, her relief changing to fear as the power flickered once again. She sat, breathing quickly, her eyes wider than ever as she stared at the silhouetted figure standing in the doorway. Yasmin lifted her shaking right hand and prepared herself to push on the device, to beg for help, to beg for anything but her impending fate.

She quickly ran her hand over the device, placed her finger over the button and pushed. A loud buzz of radio static emanated from the machine and her stalker shrieked in response, hurtling towards her. Yasmin burst in to tears as it rapidly approached her. Closing her eyes, she screamed into the headset.

Chapter 1

The morning sun shone brightly into the bedroom as the curtains were drawn back, Emily winced as the room transitioned from its darkened state. Tying the curtains up on their hooks, she took a deep breath as she turned to face the chaos.

"Jesus Christ!" she muttered under her breath.

Before her lay what could only be described as a wall of toys. She put her hand to her mouth and frowned in complete dismay, placing her hands on her hips, "Do I talk to myself or what? I. . ." she stopped herself just in time as she was greeted by her son, five-year-old Kyle.

"Morning Mum!" he smiled as he waded through the mess, side stepping, with great precision, the piles of cars, bricks, books and the like, "I just forgot my jumper."

Emily watched in annoyance as the toys parted, a little like the Red Sea, her son paying no attention to the mess, "Oh don't mind me, I'm just tidying up. . . again."

Kyle calmly opened the wooden wardrobe and pulled a green jumper from inside, "Oh thanks Mum, I just had no time to tidy it up," his voice partially muffled as he became engulfed in the jumper he was attempting to put on, one arm finding a sleeve, the other half not so much. Emily gritted her teeth and pulled the jumper down with a tug revealing the boy's innocent smile.

"Thanks Mum!" he grabbed her around her waist and squeezed gently before making a run for the stairs.

Emily shook her head, but she couldn't help a small smile for her affectionate son. She turned and calmly left the room, she was not ready to face the onslaught of cars, building blocks, teddy bears and god knows what else that could be buried beneath it all. Not right now. She stepped up into her bedroom and sat on the edge of the bed. Turning she grabbed a hair band, twisting it over and over, before pulling her hair tightly into a ponytail. The sudden quiet almost put her at ease as she prepared herself mentally for the day ahead. The chaos of their daily routine over the last few weeks had taken a real toll on the family. Emily shook her head as she thought about the ongoing saga. Her phone buzzed as she received a message. Glancing at it, she read,

Matt: Be careful out there. Something is wrong. Stay Safe.

The tone of the message from her brother really bothered her as she stared at it and reread it repeatedly. Her brother worked for the local government sector and had recently hurriedly installed a panic room into the family's basement, designed to his specifications. When the town's sudden military lockdown came, he insisted they have it fitted - no reason given, no questions asked, he just wouldn't allow it. It had to be done.

Emily remembered that day, how she'd felt completely numb when she learned that her brother was so desperate he'd felt it necessary to build her a place of safety, in her own home, in some small, unexciting town. Her neighbours were curious and, as all neighbours do, talked amongst themselves - but mostly about all the noise that shook the street for the ensuing few days.

Before she could reply to her brother's message her husband, Jack, peered around the door,

"Hey it's eight thirty, you ready? I got the kids ready for you."

"Oh yeah, I'm coming now, thanks." Emily stood and took her jacket from the hook and pulled it on as she peered down the stairs, "Jack can you make sure you finish building that stuff in the room please?"

"Yeah, I was going to anyway," he replied with a stutter, half twisting on the stairs as he looked up at her like a lost puppy.

Emily sighed, "Jack you said that last week. I mean it, it needs building." She descended the stairs as Jack began to move away. She pulled on his arm, "I'm scared."

Jack stopped mid-step and looked into her eyes; he could sense her fear just from the look she gave him. Jack smiled, climbing back up the stairs slowly, in a calming fashion, and wrapped his arms around his wife. "I will, I promise. Don't worry, I'm going to get it done."

Emily half smiled, she really was scared, nothing was making sense, but she had to be strong. They continued down the stairs and went into the living room. Emily glanced around and caught sight of the wooden pallet which leaned against the wall beside the chimney breast. She scratched her neck uneasily. She hated the state of the place, the way it made her feel.

As Jack waited for the machine to power up, he turned and picked up the TV remote control, beginning to cycle through the channels before landing on the news. He picked up the mug of coffee from the table and slouched like a teenager on the arm of the chair. As he sipped the hot drink, he squirmed uncomfortably as he watched the TV which hung above the fireplace on their wall.

"There is more to this than you're telling us, isn't there?"

"Absolutely not, the military presence is a precaution."

"Against what? The biohazard?"

"It's purely make-believe, there is-"

Emily pulled on Jack's arm and shot him a hard glare, "Can you at least wait till the kids are out?" Jack quickly looked down at his son who was staring at the TV.

"Dad, what's a biohazard?" the voice asked from the doorway.

Jack turned again to find his daughter standing there with an uneasy look on her face. "It's nothing Amy." Jack hit the power button on the remote and swung off the chair, leaning down to his daughter, "Just grown men talking sh-"

Emily bumped him in the hip, "About a movie. Now let's get you two out of here. Dad has got lots to do on his own and you two have a school to attend." Emily gently nudged Kyle towards the door with her hand, pushing gently on his little shoulder and giving a twisting hand gesture to Amy, who rolled her eyes and slumped towards the door. Emily leaned back to check her children had headed to the door before grabbing her husband and gently kissing his lips. She stepped back and smiled, giving a gentle wave as she headed out herself.

"Okay, Danger Duo. Masks on please, you know the drill."

Emily and Amy pulled on their masks, each of them twisting the small dial, the LED lighting up green beside the filter which sat on the side. Emily leaned down to her son who began tapping his foot and struggling with his own face mask. "Hey, let me help you." She held his hand and helped pull the mask over his small ears. Despite the mask, Emily smiled and ruffled his hair before twisting the dial on her son's mask and reaching for the door handle. "Okay, we're off now see you later. Don't break anything!" her speech muffled behind her mask. Her husband chuckled and gave the trio a wave as they headed out.

Stepping down onto the front street, Emily took a deep breath as she prepared herself for the school run. Placing her hands on Kyle's shoulders, Emily then took hold of his small hand as she guided him down the street, feeling his fear through the tightness of his grip on her hand. As they walked, she gently rubbed her fingers over his to comfort him. To her right, Amy walked with her head down to avoid any unnecessary human contact on her trip to school.

Reaching the end of their street they were immediately met with a checkpoint, its high fencing and the worn army green tarp towering over them. The queue of people attempting to get through was already long. Following the fence down, the soldiers and checkpoint guards stood tall and powerful before them. This part never got any easier. They had been doing this for the last few weeks. Every time Emily became extremely agitated with the soldiers, the clunking of their rifles as they paced between the various lines that formed gave her no feeling of safety.

"Passes at the ready. Move along once you have been checked. Do not attempt to rush," the checkpoint guard commanded at the head of the long queue. The guard stepped forward, his rifle glinting in the sunshine despite its jet-black paint. Emily gulped and felt herself squeezing her son's hand, she put her arm around Amy as they began to slowly move forward. All around them people were shuffling forward, herded like sheep. Everybody kept their head down, trying not to make eye contact. The gentle beep of the scanners held by the checkpoint guards became a steady rhythm interrupting the murmurs of the tense crowd. Emily jolted as an arm flailed out in front of her. Glancing up with her eyes wide, she met the hard stare of the guard,

"Your pass," he demanded once again.

Emily nodded. Unwrapping her daughter from her iron grip, she slipped her phone from her pocket and tapped the passcode. A QR code covered the screen. The guard pulled the trigger on his scanner illuminating her phone with a red light for a moment. He held his arm in place with a firm fist. "Hold," he glanced up from the screen and back to the scanner several times. The agonising delay whilst they waited for the passcode to register was almost unbearable under the soldier's intense gaze. Eventually, the phone shone a bright green covering the soldier's mask. Without a word, he stepped aside and ushered them through before calling for the next person to come forward. Emily crammed the phone back into her pocket and almost pushed her children over in her hurry to get through the checkpoint.

Brushing past the tarp she hurried into the next zone and would have carried on at pace to the school had Kyle not begun to grumble. Emily looked down and caught his eye. She slowed and stopped as a military truck roared past them, scratching the already damaged tarmac as it clattered over the speed humps. giving her a moment to shake off the fear, "Okay, so what are you guys doing today?"

"Surviving another awful day!" Amy glanced up at her mum who glared in return.

"Okay, good chat, and what about you Kyle, I bet you'll be playing with your friends as usual?"

Kyle squeezed his Mum's hand and gently nodded. Emily got down to one knee and lifted her son's head, "Hey it's going to be okay; I promise."

"Mum you can-," Amy grunted as Emily elbowed her and

returned another hard stare warning her to stop. Shaking her head, Amy huffed and slowly began to walk ahead, joining another queue. Glancing back, she rolled her eyes again and waved her arm, urging them to hurry,

"Hey Kyle, remember that cat we used to see on our way to school, that one with the cute socks?"

Kyle gripped her hand tightly, "Oh yeah, he had an odd number of socks Mum, he had three!"

"That's right!"

"I hope he isn't gone." Kyle immediately stopped his cheerful recollection as he stared off into the distance. Emily sighed, shook her head and gently pulled her son as they crossed the road and joined the queue for the school checkpoint.

The school run which used to be so simple had now become a real chore for them. The numerous checkpoints meant there was a constant stop-start motion, and the chaos was unrelenting. For weeks this had gone on and despite being told it would end soon, the time spent at the checkpoints only took longer as everybody was temperature-checked and scanned. Everyone continued to insist it was a precaution for something wild like space fuel. Emily wished somebody would just give her something real for once, rather than the lies even those telling them didn't believe. As she stood in the queue, surrounded by the embodiment of impatience she was suddenly called to the second checkpoint and her children were guided forwards by the commanding hand gesture of the next guard. This part they had to do alone, much to Kyles's horror. Emily stood, tears welling up behind her eyes, as the guard raised his palm signalling for the family to stop.

"The boy first," the guard commanded as he ushered Kyle over with his gloved fist, his rifle swinging to his side.

Kyle turned and stared at his mother with wide eyes as she nodded giving him the permission he needed to bravely step forward.

"Go on, it'll be okay. Be brave for me."

Kyle slowly turned and began to move.

"Come on kid, we can't wait," the guard ordered impatiently, banging the table with his fist.

Kyle jumped up and timidly stepped forward listening to the guard's instructions. Despite having done this over and over, the fear inside him never eased. There was no chance to hop and skip to the school gate, no time to admire the garden on the way and spy the brightly coloured butterflies flapping easily in the gentle breeze. No, the beeps of the temperature guns, the rattle of the assault rifles and the loud mutterings filling the air displaced all sense of happiness from his body. The guard stepped back and pointed to the gate's exit. Kyle stepped out of the checkpoint and stood just to the right, leaning against the fencing as his mother had told him to do, to stay in sight through the wire fence while they followed his little footsteps.

"Next." The guard tapped the temperature gun against the table and pointed to Amy who, for all her bravado, stumbled forward, the command ringing in her ears as she moved toward the guard. The ritual continued, the beep, the bright light against her forehead and the attempt to smile at her little brother who stood so bravely to one side. Despite everything going on, she always looked after her little brother. He was a sweet little thing who always wanted to talk to her, she enjoyed being his go-to buddy. She acted as a bodyguard for him. Amy felt, now more than ever, she needed to be bold - much to her parents' dismay - but it helped to ground her through the disheartening chaos that surrounded them all.

As always, the guard laid out his arms and ushered her through, another moment to push to the back of her mind as she sped up and embraced her brother who let out a small whimper as she reached him. Emily smiled beneath her mask.

"Next." The repetition continued as the man commanded Emily to step forward and she obliged him. She stood in front of the guard maintaining the ritual as he put the gauge to her head and pulled the trigger. As she stood there, the world around her suddenly shifted.

As if in slow motion, the guard released the gauge, the bright red light flickering off. He gave a horrified, wide-eyed look as the device left his hand and clattered against the floor. Emily was abruptly moved out of the way and found herself nearly face down, leaning against an iron table, its contents falling and rattling around her as the world became unusually muffled.

The guards were moving, not as a well-trained unit, but in staggered chaos as the checkpoint descended into something of a riot. People were barging, screaming, weaving between each other, without direction. Her grip slowly tightened against the table as her breathing became fast and heavy. Unable to move, she watched as the guards merged with the surrounding soldiers, their weapons raised forward with commitment, though this did not stop the crowd from pushing through them with zero thought. The soldiers forcibly shoved the crowd aside, shouting for them to move. As the crowd parted, a man stood in a starfish shape and shook violently, his body releasing a horrendous, deep groan. It came not from his mouth but from his body. Without warning, his body rippled, his arm snapped violently downwards detaching itself. Replacing it was a long, dark tentacle which swung out across the guards, batting them away with aggression and ease. The shouting did not cover the ear-splitting scream emitted by the man who arrived as quickly as the guards fell. Emily's own eyes widened in horror as something was sprinting towards them. A long, grey object dragged itself across the floor, knocking away anything in its path with amazing force. She winced and found herself something to use as a weapon. The object continued to move towards her. Emily roused herself and gripped the object with all her might, swinging as hard as she could, hitting it across its face. A dark liquid sprayed across her and the makeshift weapon she was wielding dropped from her hand as she stumbled backwards into the table. She stared at the human-like creature which shook on the floor, it's mouth spewing liquid, the smell of which could only be described as being like rotting flesh. Emily wretched as she turned gripping the table once again.

"Mum!"

She glanced up at her children who had remained standing in the same place, just to the right of the fence as they would on any other day, screaming, tears running down their faces. Emily side-stepped the table and ran towards them. Bending on one knee, she grabbed them both, holding them as tightly as she could. She leaned back as her son stuttered, fumbling for words, only managing to point. Turning, she caught the chaos for a moment and grabbed both of their hands.

"Move, come on!"

She dragged them across the street. Crowds of people ran in every direction as Emily, Amy and Kyle weaved between them. Emily stopped as she reached the other side, her surroundings were a complete blur as she spun around, spying a way out. As she turned, she was close enough to her daughter's school to see the large entrance sign hanging overhead.

"Let's go, we can get inside the school!"

She pushed the children ahead and up the ramp. As they reached the door they were met with a barricade.

"No, no, no, help us please!" she screamed as the three of them pounded their fists on the glass door. She was taken aback by the figure who appeared before them.

"Hey, let us in please. I have children!"

He moved closer to the glass and shook his head. Emily scowled as he denied them entry,

"Open this door now!" Emily barged the door with her shoulder and the man stepped back, the light revealing his face.

"Hey, you're her teacher, don't you fucking leave us out here!"

The man shook his head again and stepped back.

"Don't you dare! You bastard, you open this door, you're going to kill us!"

The man stopped, and appeared to shout, before stepping to the door and pulling a large metallic object from it, allowing the three of them into the safety of the dark entrance.

"Get the door!" he shouted as he pushed the double doors closed, Emily spun round and stepped back to the door to help hold it closed as another of the monsters charged towards it.

"Amy, grab that bar now!" she called, holding her hand out. Amy stumbled over to the bar and passed it like a baton to her mother, who squeezed it between the metal door handles. The pair stepped back, glancing at each other with wide eyes. The monster continued to charge the door before pressing its deformed face against the glass, screaming as it moved back before charging back into the chaos of the crowded streets. Emily fell backwards, finding the entrance hall wall and collapsing, feeling the comfort of the hard, black carpet beneath her. Taking in a deep breath, Emily closed her eyes and desperately tried to hold back the tears. Her world was about to come crashing down around her.

Chapter 2

Emily slowly opened her eyes. Raising her arm, she used the sleeve of her jacket to wipe away a rogue tear; she still found herself in complete shock. Glancing up she saw that the man who had almost left them outside to die in the chaos, was kneeling down, talking to her children.

"So, you do have a heart," she called sarcastically as she slowly pushed herself to stand.

"Listen, I. . ."

"No, kids come here." Emily held out her arms and embraced her children, their own emotions getting the better of them as they burst into tears and launched into a barrage of questions.

"Mum, what's going on? I don't get it, why's everyone going crazy?" Amy peeled away from her mother's arms, tears flowing down her cheeks, "And what's that on your face?"

Emily turned and stared at her own reflection in the nearest glass cabinet, leaning in close. Her eyes widened as she saw the black mess splattered across her face and jacket, the stain spreading from her face to her chest and then to her arm, but the smell was what suddenly hit her senses. Emily frantically peeled the jacket from her body, feeling the weight of it slide from her as it dropped to the floor. She began to scrub at her face vigorously as she attempted to clean off the mess. As she did so, something began battering the door again and the four of them spun round and edged slowly backwards.

"Come on, the others are in the main hall, we should head inside." The teacher held Emily's shoulders and pointed calmly, "We should really be inside by now. Kids, show your Mum the main hall."

The sound of the creature's slamming fists felt like a drum inside Emily's head. She shook as she followed them out of the entrance hall, the sound becoming muffled as she headed deeper into the school. They headed down a long, narrow corridor, its walls covered in the pupils' artwork. The atmosphere became darker, and the neat cuttings more twisted and torn, the further inside they went. Emily glanced at the floor, unsure where to look as the chaos seemed to follow her, the paper scrabbling like little hands at her arms as she walked.

As they reached the hall the teacher peered through the window and waved. Another wide-eyed face appeared.

"Mrs Fay!" Kyle shouted as he pulled on his Mum's arm, "That's Mrs Fay."

The door clunked as the teacher pulled something from behind it and swung open. The four of them rushed inside, the teacher squeezing the barrier back against the door and then swinging round to embrace Kyle.

"Oh Kyle, I'm so glad you're safe!"

"I am, Mrs Fay. My Mum saved us, she hit the thing like a superhero!" he exclaimed as he pulled away from his teacher, "Mum was really brave."

Mrs Fay glanced up and stared at Emily, the look on the mother's face spoke volumes about the situation, "Mrs Farragher, I hate to say it, but you look awful."

Emily cracked half a smile beneath her mask, but it didn't

last. "I feel it." She slowly turned around and examined the hall they'd hurried into. Few people had sought safety in the school hall, she'd expected to find more children, their parents and any others who had managed to get in. She counted the heads in the room, the ones who were lucky. Were they lucky? She wandered further towards those taking refuge and paused as the sound of text notifications gently echoed round the room.

As she stepped into the crowd, she caught one of the other parents fumbling around with a smartphone. Stepping closer, she jumped as someone shouted,

"Yeah, I got it too. Wait, there's audio! Right listen, I'll put the volume up. Tell everyone to quieten down."

"Everyone shut up, we've got something over here!"

Emily stood, surprised by the response from the crowd, and found herself joining in. She leaned towards a man holding out a smartphone. On the screen was the logo used by the British Government. She jumped again as the smartphone began to read aloud the text that appeared on the screen, the voice robotic.

"This is a British Government announcement. A class 1 emergency has been declared in your area. Seek immediate safety. Do not leave your home, lock all windows and doors. Wear and activate your S.F.M. Do not leave your home unless instructed to by British Army personnel. An airborne virus is active in your area. Symptoms include a high fever, black oily excretion, extreme muscle pain and fatigue. Anyone displaying these symptoms should isolate immediately until further notice. Do not call emergency services."

The message began to repeat. The man holding the smartphone lowered the volume, unwilling to listen to the instructions again. The room fell quiet, people holding each other tighter, small whimpers cracking the uneasy silence.

"Here please, sit. You look like you might fall over." Mrs Fay brought a chair over and gently lowered Emily into it, "Let me get you some water, hold on." She wandered off to the kitchen behind the hall as Emily put her head in her hands and breathed heavily. Her children sat down beside her, she clutched them once more.

"Kids. whatever happens, we're going to make it, we're going to get out of this." She found the strength to really smile this time. The children smiled back, their eyes revealing their emotions. She hoped she'd given them a moment of comfort.

"Mum, wait. What about Dad? Is he okay?"

"Shit! Sorry, where's my phone?" Emily patted her pockets violently, trying to find her smartphone. Suddenly, it dawned on her that her phone was outside in the pocket of the jacket that she left in the entrance hall. Emily rose quickly and sprinted for the barricaded door.

"Wait, Mrs Farragher! What are you. . ?" The teacher rose to challenge her, but Emily had already reached the barricade. As she began to remove it, she abruptly came to a halt. She stared through the window, frozen in place. Mrs Fay slowed to a walk and stepped toward her.

"Mrs Fa-" As she began to question Emily's intentions, the teacher turned to look out of the window and found the reason her mission had been paused. She pulled on Emily's arm and gradually began to move back, taking the concerned parent with her. A few steps and it began again, the wild thudding, the drumming battering her senses. Emily turned,

"I'm-" She could say no more, the continuous banging filled her with total fear. The hall filled with fearful screams and shouts of commands as everyone moved away from the doorway.

Emily found she was unable to move at more than a crawl as she stepped slowly away. A small hand pulled her to the side as the heavy pounding stopped, the metal barricade dropped, and the chaos ensued once again. The monster screamed into the hall, its body deformed, its human features barely visible behind the pulsing liquid covering its body. Two pairs of little hands pulled Emily away from the door

and on to her back. The three of them found themselves scrabbling across the cold floor, the monster inching towards them, flailing with aggression. As they dragged themselves away, they found their backs to the kitchen wall. They were completely stuck with nowhere to go. Emily grabbed her children and closed her eyes. The sound of a metal bar hitting flesh soon shook her eyes open. Looking up she found Mrs Fay standing over them.

"Come on, we have to go!" She held out her arm and helped Emily and her children up, turning she stared in disbelief at the horror in front of her.

"Where are we going?" Emily asked, "We have to go, we can't help them."

Mrs Fay turned and pushed them through the door to the kitchen. As it closed, she pulled the large milk cage in front of the door and used her foot to push the wheel brakes on. Not much of a barricade but at least it was something to slow them down. Emily tugged Mrs Fay's arm again, "I'm sorry for what I did but we have to move now!"

Mrs Fay turned, no longer in teacher mode, "What were you thinking? What was so damned important you had to get out?" She pulled Emily in closer, "You. . ." she stopped as she noticed the children staring too.

Emily grabbed Mrs Fay's arm and peeled it off her own, "What does it matter?" Standing up straight, she pulled her children closer again, "It was stupid, but we're alive, now can we please keep moving or do you have something more to say to me?" Mrs Fay huffed and barged past, pressing her back to the wall. Emily gently nudged her children onwards. Mrs Fay pulled the handle, opening the door which led into the main corridor. She peered through the gap and edged the door open further until she could turn her head left to right.

"Follow me. We should get to one of the upper classrooms, we can hide in the back of the school. No one was up that way, it should be safe. . . I hope."

Emily nodded and the four of them headed down the corridor, their backs to the wall as they carefully moved further into the school. The distant screaming from the hall echoed around them and the children jumped at the bumps. Their mother guided them as gently as possible behind their teacher. As they turned a corner, Emily paused briefly and glanced back. She felt nothing but despair, she didn't dare imagine what the aftermath of their escape would be. Kyle pulled on her arm and guided her back to their teacher who ushered them on. Emily knew she couldn't afford to think of the others, her children were what mattered now, their safety depended on her. She had to stay calm. As they reached another junction, Mrs Fay turned and pulled Amy to the front,

"Amy, I need you to take your brother up the stairs here."

"No Miss. Please, I don't want to go without you and Mum," Amy trembled.

"Hey, it's okay. We'll be right behind you. You two need to get in first for us." Mrs Fay held Amy's shoulders, a smile showing in her eyes, "Be brave," she turned to Emily, "like your mum." Amy nodded and held Kyles's hand. She slowly began to climb the stairs. Kyle held his mother's gaze; all she could do was nod at him just as she'd done back at the checkpoint.

The two women moved towards the stairs hearing the clatter of metal and the roar of the crowd as they were released from the main hall. In a matter of seconds, any last trace of calmness evaporated. As the situation escalated, the two children screamed. Emily sped down the corridor and peered round the corner. At the other end of the corridor all was in chaos. Blood soaked the carpets as a mass of stumbling bodies tried to escape, fleeing wildly in all directions. As she tried to fight the urge to be sick, two of the monsters emerged from amongst the bodies.

They shook uncontrollably as they sank to the ground, screaming, transforming their bodies, and reacting in the same way as the man at the checkpoint had done when he had changed. Emily found herself transfixed by the horrific scene as each body seemed to twist and break as if it was transforming into something else entirely. As the show finished, one of the creatures looked directly at Emily and began to move like a hound to blood, darting nearly on all fours. Were it not impeded by the thin replacement it had growing from where its previous arm had been, the monster's speed would have been impressive. Emily jolted backwards and moved towards her children and the teacher.

"Go! They're coming!"

Mrs Fay turned to the children and pointed down the corridor. "You two go! Run to the end and go into the very last classroom, now!" The children nodded and sped down the corridor, the pair of them moving as quickly as possible. Kyle glanced back to see what was happening but Amy tugged on his arm.

"Come on we have to go!" she shouted,

"But mum she. . ."

"No, come on. You heard Mrs Fay, we have to get inside!" Amy slowed as she reached the end classrooms, deciding which to enter, before trying any handle. To her relief the one she picked opened under the weight of her hand. Amy stepped inside.

"Okay Kyle, help me move this table, we need. . ." Amy peered over the table, "Kyle?"

As she side-stepped the table, her heart beat rapidly in her chest. As Kyle carefully moved into the classroom, the monster lurched around, placing its body in front of the open doorway. Its extended arms scratched at the door frame, chipping away at the paintwork. Its voice cracked between high and low pitch, it's body still twitching as it appeared to eye up her brother. She raised her hands to her face as she saw the creature's eyes widened. She found herself frozen in place through pure fear. As she fought to move her body, the monster let out a muffled scream as it became covered by a cloud of smoke. As it received a stream of blasts from the fire extinguisher, it dropped to the floor, repeatedly slamming its head against it. Through the smoke, Emily stepped up. Amy screamed and jumped for her, squeezing her tightly around her waist.

"Mum, you're okay!"

"It's alright, we're here." Emily turned and found Mrs Fay firing the remainder of the fire extinguisher's contents directly against the monster's battered head before throwing it aside, trying to catch her breath.

"Let's get this door closed. . . now. Push the desk up against it and I'll grab something to cover the window." She stumbled inside and closed the door behind her. Emily, Kyle and Amy worked as one to move the desk against it. Mrs Fay ripped a poster from the wall display and clambered over the desk, placing the poster over the window.

"Tape," she pointed to the stationery box tucked under the counter, "Amy, the tape please." Amy ran to the counter, pulling out the drawers with such force, the materials flew from their neat arrangement and were strewn across the floor. Grabbing the tape, she weaved between the desks and handed it over. Stepping back and breathing deeply, she watched her teacher rip pieces of the tape off one by one to attach the poster to the door.

The four of them slowly clambered from their positions and stepped back. They stopped, finding themselves frozen, unable to move for fear another monster would batter down the door and discover them. Eventually, Emily reached out and pulled her children towards her, hugging them tightly. She tried to talk, to say anything, but just squeaks came out. She buried her head into their shoulders, for what felt like hours to her children. Mrs Fay turned and faced the trio.

"We should stay here for now." She glanced at the door and stood, ruffling Kyle's hair slightly, "We're going to be okay."

Emily lifted her head and watched as the teacher moved into the room, placing her hands on the counter at the back of the classroom. Slouching, exhausted and beaten from the morning's chaos, she collapsed and began to sob.

Emily kissed her children on the head and rose. "Guys, can you just give me a minute?" She nodded to their broken teacher, "I'm going to go over and see how she's doing. Why don't you show your sister how to draw those dinosaurs like your Dad showed you?"

"Oh, Amy they're so cool, they have little hands and super big feet and they do like to eat pies!" Kyle's eyes lit up as he looked over at his sister, her eyes rolled, but she smiled,

"Okay Kyle, go grab some paper and some pencils. We can maybe help them to be a little nicer to each other." Kyle crossed the room and grabbed the pencil case which had fallen from the teacher's desk in all the madness. Emily smiled as the pair of them began to enjoy drawing together. Her smile fell as she stepped between the children's desks, she had no idea what she was going to do or was going to say to them. How she could do anything for her children's teacher? She had saved their lives but she'd nearly killed them in the process. Emily noticed an unopened packet of paper towels, grabbing a handful, she held them out, smiling awkwardly as she offered them to Mrs Fay. The pair stared at each other for a moment, their hands identical in the way the dark liquid from the monsters they'd beaten was now stained on their skin like a tattoo. Mrs Fay found herself simply squeezing the towels before walking off and sitting on one of the children's chairs, staring once again into oblivion. Emily turned away trying not to make things any more difficult. The sounds of the dying echoed around and inside the room. Her children sat drawing, smiling, taking a moment away from the strange madness. Surely this was not to be their new normal.

Chapter 3

Emily quietly and carefully laid her son's head on the jacket they had found inside the classroom. The classroom had become their new shelter and now night-stop. Steadily, she stretched over Amy who had been sprawled out against her leg. Once free, she crept over to the teacher who was sitting with her back to the wall, wide awake.

"Hey," Emily whispered.

"Hey."

"Thank you for, err, what you did earlier."

Mrs Fay looked up expressionlessly, "I don't know what I did really, but I do know it was something wrong. It's just so... wrong. I don't even know what came over me. I just hit the thing, whatever it is and. . ."

"I know how you feel," Emily glanced at her children, "On our way in we got to the school checkpoint then, suddenly, the world just stopped. I felt like I had lost my hearing, the noise just went like that. I was attacked by one, but before. . . before that, this person just changed, he changed in front of me. It was like some insane sci-fi movie."

Emily quivered a little and started to pick at her fingernails, "In a flash it ran at me and I. . . hit it. I somehow grabbed this metal bar and hit it so hard it screamed. The noise. . . it was like it could feel it. I just turned and ran for these two and, well, you know the rest. Ha, I don't even know your first name."

"It's Janet, and I appreciate the heart to heart, but I can't bear to think about it - well I am but I don't want to. It's not human, it's not something we should be doing, I'm a teacher. God knows what you do, but as a mother your instinct is to protect, teachers have that too, maybe that's what it was, a maternal instinct."

"I'm not sure but however we spin this, I think our moral compass is now fucked." The women laughed a little. The children moved slightly, and the pair stopped, glancing back at each other they laughed again.

"Oh, what are we going to do?" Emily tilted her head and leaned against the wall. "We have no way out and no way of contacting anyone."

She turned back and found Janet scrabbling around on her hands and knees, "What are you doing?"

"Ah ha," Janet shuffled back and presented Emily with their only option, "Why don't we figure it out together courtesy of a confiscated phone?"

Emily took the phone and pushed the power button, the screen lit up the room. She quickly began dragging her finger across the screen and adjusted the brightness to something less like a strobe light. As she settled in and wondered what to do, she spotted the extremely low percentage across the top of the screen.

"Err, what child doesn't charge their phone up these days?"

"Look, what's that message at the top?" Emily pulled down from the screen and a message appeared on it -

You are in a Class 1 crisis zone. Your local government have designated the following safe zones at – Drayton Library, Drayton Town Hall (Crisis Centre) and Drayton Highway Bunker. Stay indoors. Do not leave under any circumstances unless directed to by military personnel.

Janet leaned away from the screen and smiled, a real smile this time.

"The library isn't far. It's about five minutes down the main road. If we move slowly enough, we should get there easily. It's dark and it's really quiet out there now."

Emily nodded, "Sounds like an idea. Do we even know how to get in? I thought I heard about passes and things."

"I don't see why not. Surely, they must let us in, we're local and not exactly breaking any rules or laws. It's a shelter. They have to let us in."

Janet quietly got to her feet and gestured with her hand against her ear, "Why don't you try to make that call you wanted to make this morning?"

She smiled and headed over to the children as Emily sat staring at the screen. That call. The call she was so desperate to make and now she could. She tapped the icons and brought up the number pad, the low battery warning covering the screen. Emily quickly tapped the screen to move the message on and began to type in her husband's phone number, finally hitting the call button. She held the phone to her ear, the call tone possibly the most pleasant sound she had heard in the last few hours. Her small smile didn't last long as the phone kept ringing out until the standard, boring voicemail request began to run its speech. Her throat dried and she found herself breathing heavily, barely noticing the tone to begin leaving a message.

"Jack. . . I. . . I hope you're okay. I-We're okay, me, the er kids, we're safe at their school. I just. . . I need to know you're okay. I lost my phone and erm I found this one but it's running low. We're heading to the library, there's a shelter there. Please if you hear this, meet us there. We need you. Please be safe. I love you."

As she clicked the icon to cancel the call, the phone flickered, and the screen went black. Dead, like the outside world. Emily placed the phone on the ground and clenched her fist tightly. As she tried to calm herself the mood became uneasy, and a slow and gentle knock began to come from the classroom door.

She rose quietly but with some urgency. Janet turned, her face pale and the knock came again. Slightly louder yet not quite regular, it sounded like somebody was unsure of what they were doing. Again, it came. The women leaned down and shook the children awake. They both awoke with a shock, but they had their mouths covered as one knock boomed within the classroom. Janet guided Amy behind her and held her hand up to stop Emily as she herself crept forward.

"Hello, is anyone there?"

There was another knock in reply and a raspy voice responded, "Yessss Janet, it'sss James."

Janet paused and her face became tight, "James? What are you doing out there?"

"I wantttt to commmme in," the voice answered as the heavy, slow pounding on the door began again.

"James, whatever's wrong? You need to stop knocking like that. Are you hurt?"

Janet began to move towards the door.

"If you are, then let me open up, we can help you."

She stepped up to the door and clambered up onto the desk, "James stand in front of the door so I can. . ." As Janet finished her request, she peeled the poster from the window and was met with a deep, broken smile. She screamed, stumbled backwards, and fell to the floor. The smile changed to a glare and whatever was outside let out a piercing scream.

"Shit, he's one of them!"

Emily pulled her children close again and helped Janet to her feet. The monster pounded harder and harder against the door, the desk blockade edging closer towards the group inside the classroom.

"I don't understand. If that's James, how is he so big?" Janet asked as she hastily searched for something to use as a weapon which, unsurprisingly, didn't present itself in the safety of a children's classroom.

The monster pounded repeatedly against the door, eventually pushing its long, thick arm through the gap, and then forcing its head through too. As James' now mutated body squeezed grotesquely through the doorway, it began to shake violently, the door slamming against the desk as it used its entire body to move the blockade and get inside. The four of them stepped back and the children huddled closer into Emily's arms, their screams matching the monster's own ear-splitting screech. They watched on in horror as James managed to slowly move the desk away from the door, incredible strength in his body.

"It'ssss tiiime fooor classs kidsss," his voice switching between various pitches as he continued to push away everything in his path.

As he began to get closer, Emily pulled her children behind her and grabbed a chair.

"Get behind me now!" Emily turned and confronted her children's, now completely deformed, teacher. "Alright James ju-just stop!"

Their teacher continued to move forward.

"I-I don't want to hurt. . ." as she tried to reason with the deformed teacher, James whipped a table away forcing it into the wall, leaving a deep gouge. Kyle and Amy screamed even more loudly, and Emily lurched forward. With all her strength, she slammed the chair across James' head. Emily released her grip on the chair as it made contact with the creature, completely caving in the monster's head. The monster dropped suddenly and the same dark liquid that had covered Emily and Janet earlier oozed from the wound, its odious smell causing Emily to gag.

"We're leaving now!" Emily held out a hand and Kyle darted forward and grabbed hold. "Kyle go, I'll be right behind you. Amy come on let's go!" Emily gently pushed Kyle on and held out her hand again as Amy stepped forward. She tried hard not to look at the monster her mother had just beaten but couldn't quite resist. Her eyes widened as she glimpsed the black liquid that was slowly covering the classroom floor, the teacher's facial features a caved-in mess.

"Amy, eyes on me, don't look at it, come on let's go!" Emily grabbed Amy, who still couldn't take her eyes off her teacher. Janet moved quickly behind her and hurried her along.

"Come on, Amy, it's over, let's go. We need to get out of here." Janet took Amy's hand and stepped out of the classroom. Emily moved for the door, stopping briefly to look back at the black-stained whiteboard, and thought of her husband. What if he came here? He knew they could be here. She had to leave some kind of trail., something to give him hope. She quickly moved through the broken chairs and fumbled for the marker pen; Janet turned in bewilderment.

"Emily, what the hell are you doing?" Janet questioned, trying to keep her voice low.

"If Jack comes looking for us, he has to know where we're going!" She pulled the lid from the marker and began to write –

Jack, the library. X. Emily moved away and dropped the marker, admiring her handwriting on the board. As they exited the classroom, another scream filled the corridor and she stared at Janet, looking for a plan. Janet shook her head and moved for the door behind them.

"Emily, there." She grabbed the bar across the fire door and pointed to the red and white fire panel next to her shoulder, "When I open this door, hit that button. We can use the sound to distract them while we make a run for it."

Emily wandered to the button and turned hesitantly, "Will this work?"

Janet pushed the bar and the fire door swung open, "Yes, now do it!" She held Kyle's shoulder and pushed him through the doorway, Amy followed. When she nodded at Emily, she used her elbow to trigger the fire alarm. Despite being aware of what she was doing, she still jumped slightly as the alarm rang out, the sound echoing across the open street.

"Come on, we should head to the library, it's our best bet." Janet grabbed Emily and pulled her along, the four of them began to jog down the pavement. As they travelled along, the aftermath of the incident was clear to see. Those unfortunate enough not to have made it out lay strewn across the roads and pavements, brutal cuts covering their bodies, their personal belongings littering the streets. Emily couldn't help but pause as they reached the checkpoint which stood between their neighbourhood and the school.

She stopped, surveying the scene, and recalling the moment, wondering what her children must have seen. What went through their minds as they watched on while it all began? The moment she hesitated, frozen in fear, as the monster made a move for her. Did they shout for her? She remembered the feeling, her inability to move, just managing to defend herself. She couldn't do that again. She couldn't allow it to happen again, her children needed her, they needed her to protect them. She couldn't hesitate.

Janet pulled on her shoulder, interrupting her train of thought.

"Emily, I know it's tough, but we have to go now. Please. Come on!"

Emily nodded and they set back off again.

"If we go further down, we can get past the lower checkpoint. It's a straight line to the library from there. It's open so keep moving. Don't stop."

It hadn't been long since the town had been put under lockdown, but in the darkness, she felt uneasy, nothing felt familiar anymore. The lights glowing in the houses along the main road gave her an eerie feeling; the local park eliciting no happy memories, in fact the metal hoarding of the outer fence said it all. Suddenly, whatever had been let loose was as bad as they had feared. Nobody knew its origin. Nobody talked about germ warfare. It was as if someone, somewhere, knew what was happening but didn't have the means to stop it. When the incident at the docks happened, the lockdown followed, and everything came to a halt. Nowhere was safe, travel was illegal, chaos reigned supreme.

Emily quelled her emotions again, unable to look anywhere near the homes of those left behind. Crossing the last road before they would reach the library, to her surprise, lights lit up the huge building and it appeared oddly inviting. Slowing, the four of them stopped at the outer wall and stepped up the ramp. The huge wooden doors were wide open but, as they entered, the appealing atmosphere quickly faded away with the stench and scene of the chaos which lay before them. The four of them walked further inside and Emily turned, spotting her children's horrified looks as they surveyed the area.

"Kids come here, come on." Kyle and Amy darted to their mother and clung on. The library had been completely ruined. Books were scattered across the floor and hung from the metal shelving. Blood marked almost every inch of the once clean parquet flooring. Janet reached the main desk and pushed away a mound of paper revealing a crudely written sign - *Safe Zone*. Under it was an arrow pointing behind her. Janet stepped back and walked, in as straight a line as she could, through the mess to a large, wooden door. She examined it from top to bottom before grabbing the handle and pushing. The door didn't budge. She tried again, to no effect. She threw her weight against the door, still nothing. Janet turned and waved her arm, Emily and her children moved towards her.

"What?"

"I think I've found the safe zone the text talked about."

Janet glanced again at the door and found a flat pad, "Argh, I think we need a key or a card or something to get in. . . damn it!" She kicked the door and spun around, shaking her head.

"I think it's probably a key card, I remember coming here and they were using their badges to get into some of the doors in the building. There must be a spare around here."

Emily took a long look around the room and stopped at the stone staircase which spiralled upwards to the next floor.

"I have an idea, why don't we have a look around? Amy, you go with your teacher and head upstairs, see if you can help her find what we need."

Amy shook her head in disapproval.

"Listen Amy," Emily knelt down and placed her hand against

the side of her daughter's face, "it's going to be okay, I promise, but we need to do this. You can do this, be brave, okay?" Amy turned to her teacher who held out her hand.

"Come on Amy, let's go, yeah?" Janet walked over and took Amy's hand, gradually pulling her towards the staircase, Emily stood and nodded, watching as they both made their way through the library.

"Okay, big man, it's our turn." Emily grabbed Kyle's hand and pointed further into the library. "We need to go that way and find a card, okay?" Kyle followed his mother's gaze. He remembered coming here often with his parents, picking up an armful of books, usually those to do with dinosaurs because they were his favourite. He remembered visiting and attending events where he would get to sit and draw at the desks, the ones just right for little guys like him. As he turned to his mother all he felt was fear, not the excitement of wondering what he would get to take home today; in fact, he wondered if he would ever get home again. Emily knelt beside him and pulled him into her arms.

"It's going to be alright Kyle, I promise. Please we must do this, it will help us get to safety, remember?"

Kyle shrugged. That was enough of a reaction for Emily, who gently tugged on her son's arm as they ventured into the back of dark children's library. The two of them stepped carefully into the darkness, feeling their way, following the small shelves, which had once been covered in the books, which now lay scattered on the floor and all around. As they made their way through, they climbed over one of the bookshelves to clear the area and continue towards the back of the library, Emily grabbed what should have been the top of the shelf and slowly pulled herself over sideways, fumbling across the slippery book jackets which littered the floor.

"Kyle, come here, I'll help you over." Kyle tried to follow his mother but found himself frantically flailing his arms in the darkness.

"Mum! Mum! I-I can't-Where are you?"

"Here Kyle, I'm right here."

"Mum, I can't-Ah Mum help me please, help me!" In panic, he spun around and put a foot onto the fallen shelf, then falling himself, "Mum!"

"Kyle, calm down." Emily grabbed hold of him and tried to pull him out, "You're stuck, you need to stop."

By now, Kyle was terrified. He began to thrash violently against the shelving, his mother's arms and the metal bookends which once held the books in place., "Kyle, Kyle. Stop!" Emily finally got a hold on her son who was laid at a strange angle within the shelving. "Hey. . .Hey it's okay. . .Shh." She combed her fingers through his hair and began to comfort him. Kyle took several quick breaths as he found himself in a complete tangle, unsure of what to do. Once in his mother's embrace, he began to slow down. Breath by breath, he calmed, and, within minutes, he eventually stopped.

"Right, now I need you to carefully pull yourself over towards me, okay? Slowly."

"I'm s-sorry Mum," Kyle stammered as he followed his mother's instructions and pulled himself free from the shelf trap and on to her lap, "I hope the monsters don't come."

"Me too kid. Now come on, hold tight this time." Emily placed her son's arms on her hips and led the way through the exit of the children's library. She quickly found another doorway and carefully pushed it open. As they crept inside, the emergency light flickered, there was just enough light for them to be able to find their way through the debris. Emily winced each time the dimly lit exit sign flickered as she tried to find her bearings inside the small room as she glanced around. To her left stood another door but the way to it was blocked, by what, she couldn't tell. The metal shine told her it wasn't where she was going next.

She moved herself and her son to the right, closer to the desk. She stepped warily so she wouldn't come crashing down onto whatever was in the room. Her son didn't use that level of care and found himself standing on the back of Emily's shoe, causing her to lurch forward. Emily held out her arms and landed in a sprawl on the floor, her head hitting the front panelling of the desk. The two of them laid on the floor. Emily blinked hard and forced her eyes open as she looked around in panic for her son.

"Kyle! Kyle!"

"Here mum, but why aren't you moving?"

Emily quickly shuffled her body up and found herself staring at her son, "Ooooh Kyle, don't. . . Just stay there." Emily lifted onto her knees, Kyle sat on the floor in shock, "Just come here, don't turn around, okay?" As she pulled him away, she found what she was looking for, but she was also met with the slashed face of someone who had not been as fortunate as them. Emily had to place one of her free hands over her mouth and her other clumsily around her son as he slowly shuffled over. The light continued to flicker, she just about made out the lanyard around the victim's neck, with the badge still attached. Emily took a deep breath and leaned forward, "Just. . . stay there. . .Kyle, one second." She reached out her free hand and grabbed the lanyard, pulling it down quickly and disconnecting the badge. Emily guided her son backwards with her. "Let's go. Now," she ordered as she dragged Kyle through the doorway and back into the children's library. She didn't stop despite clattering into everything along the way, pulling her son through it all with her as he grumbled about the shelves he was repeatedly banging against. She couldn't stop, she had to get out of the darkness. Stepping back into the light of the main entrance, Emily grabbed onto the desk and spun round, sinking to the floor with her son buried in her arms. Janet and Amy wandered into the entrance.

"Jesus are you two. . ?"

Emily held the bloodstained lanyard as high as she could for Janet to see it before lowering it again.

"Well, I won't ask how you got that, but we should see if it works." Janet stepped over Emily and attempted to take the lanyard from her, but Emily didn't let go, Janet met her gaze with confusion.

"I'll do it." Emily pulled the lanyard back in to her possession and pushed her son up. Kyle sprang into his sister's arms and gave her an excited embrace. Stumbling to the door panel, Emily breathed in and placed the badge against the black panel, exhaling as the door panel shone a brilliant green, the thud of the lock releasing filling her with an immense joy.

The four of them found themselves staring hard into the dimly lit room, a staircase twisted around it's outer wall. Emily edged inside the doorway and peered over the railing, there wasn't much of a drop so she assumed the safe area would be just a moment away,

"Okay, well, this is it I guess." Emily tentatively entered the dark again, taking small, slow steps as the others followed suit. Her son instantly grabbed her hand and clung on tightly. The four of them moved towards the bottom of the stairs. Emily fumbled for the door handle, pulling it downwards. The light from the room inside caught her off guard, but that wasn't her biggest concern. The door handle was pulled from her grip and she found herself face to face with a taser. Kyle jolted and hid behind Emily, Janet and Amy clung to the wall in the dark of the room.

"Woah, woah, woah, hang on, I'm not a thing, a whatever."

"Don't move. Just stop!" The woman behind the taser had a steady aim, the red dot focusing on Emily's chest, suggesting that she wasn't prepared to risk anything,

"Please," she ushered Kyle to the front, "I'm-We're just looking for somewhere to hide."

"How did you even get in? You need a card to. . ." The woman took a step back and lowered her weapon slightly. In response, Emily stepped forward, but the woman raised her weapon again, "How did you get that card?"

"We found it. It was in the back of the library; I don't know where we were exactly."

"Did you find the card," the woman pressed forward slowly, "or the poor person wearing it?"

"If you're insinuating that I killed them for it, then, Jesus Christ, no. We're desperate but I'm no monster, not like whatever is out there. Please, we're scared and tired. My kids need somewhere to rest." Emily moved to the side and pulled Amy from behind the wall and into the light. The woman watched. Janet sidled in and gave an awkward wave.

"She, however, isn't a child but she did save my, I mean our, lives."

The woman stood for a moment in thought before lowering her weapon and signalling for them to step inside, allowing the door to close behind them. Emily breathed out heavily and found a hand grabbing tightly around her own.

"I'll be having that." The woman took the lanyard from Emily who quickly released her grip. She watched as it was placed on the top of the desk. Emily guided the group inside. The room wasn't huge, more of a book storage space, dozens of metal rollers followed the room from top to bottom. It had been painted white, probably to create a less imposing feeling, though time had taken its toll on the walls and patches of paint had flaked away, the dust covering the floor and the various boxes that clung to the wall. The floor was a cheap laminate, easy cleaning, which might be helpful for the dirt and blood which now stained it.

"So, how many are down here?" Emily casually asked walking over to the woman who'd let them in.

"Ten. Only ten, not including me. I'm glad of it, this place is not a damn fortress."

"But this was listed as. . ."

"It was listed, yes, but this is not somewhere you can hide for the fucking foreseeable. It's a damn basement full of, oh yeah, books! We got a supply yesterday of some water and cheap crap from the army. It'll last us barely a handful of days." The woman kicked over a stack of books as another stepped into view. "Oh Mrs Tyson, I'm sorry, did I wake you?"

Emily turned towards this woman, who she estimated must have been in her sixties, standing there clutching the metal shelf like a human bookend, "Can I get some water from you please?"

Emily turned back to the first woman, who despite having been seconds from kicking hell out of something or someone, managed a small smile beneath her mask. She pulled open one of the cardboard boxes, inside was the water she'd mentioned. She walked over calmly and handed the older woman a bottle.

"Thank you, Bethany, that's lovely," and with that she turned and wandered off. Emily followed her to the beginning of the shelves, Bethany stepped to her side.

"That's where we're all sleeping," Emily turned to face her with a raised brow, "Okay, when I'm not biting someone's head off." Bethany turned back and began to rummage in another box and produced a handful of blankets, "This is the best I can do. Grab one and head down the back. The book rollers wind back enough to give us a gap between each other, not that it matters anyway just head down and grab a row." Bethany squeezed past the four of them and headed for the sleep space. Emily followed cautiously with the others in tow, her children rushed to her side and held on to her tightly.

"Well, we made it! You can finally get some sleep."

"That would be nice, Mum, I am so tired and, well, it's been a bit scary." Kyle squeezed Emily a little and she squeezed both him and Amy.

"It has been a hell of a day. . . and night."

"I hope Dad's okay," Amy stated quietly as she held her head against her Mum, wondering if he had managed to stay safe. Emily hoped he had gone into their basement and was just lying low. Really though, she just wanted them altogether again. Hopefully somebody in the shelter would have a phone she could use to keep trying to reach Jack. Bethany patted the roller beside her and ushered the family between the large steel shelves crammed with a mixture of books, maps, and supplies.

"You three have this one," she stepped up to the teacher and ushered her back, "You have the one behind them."

Janet glanced at Emily who nodded, and the exhausted teacher twisted the iron bar to reveal her own sleeping quarters. Emily watched as Janet shuffled in between the shelves and Bethany waved, stepping away and leaving the family to settle in. The children stepped forward, taking in their surroundings; the thought of having to sleep on a cold, hard floor with just a blanket for comfort did not fill them with joy. Emily could sense the sombre mood but knew that, as their mother, she had a duty to remain positive for them.

"Come on you two," she squeezed between them and knelt on the ground. She rolled her own blanket round her arms and placed it on the ground close to the wall, "You can use me as a pillow tonight, alright?" She laid down. Kyle beamed from behind his mask as he darted into his mother's arms. Emily pulled his blanket over him and waved Amy in, "Come on, you, even you're invited." Amy cautiously stepped over and knelt down, lying next to her mother who placed an arm over her, "I told you, I'm not leaving either of you. We will be okay, I promised you, didn't I?"

Emily felt the pair of them doze off to sleep within minutes. An immense feeling of relief took over and she found herself calming, if only briefly, despite all the chaos. Before her imagination could get the better of her, she found herself drifting off to sleep as she was finally able to rest.

Chapter 4

Emily awoke from her well-earned rest, albeit with a very sore back. She rolled over and blindly patted the space where her bedside table would usually be found, instead feeling the cold, hard, steel bookshelf. She jolted upright, remembering where she was and quickly realising that her children were gone. Throwing the blanket to the side, she rapidly stepped over the metal rails she had barely noticed the previous night, and out into the basement corridor.

"Kyle! Amy!" She stumbled down the corridor shouting again, "Kids?" As she moved further down a man stepped out from a gap between the rollers and grabbed her,

"What the hell are you shouting for?" The man let her go but blocked her path.

"I'm looking for my children, have you. . ." As she peered behind him, a little face peaked out from the furthest shelf and greeted her with happy eyes.

"Mum look!" Kyle held out a book and waved it happily, "It's my favourite book!"

Emily pushed past the confused man and grabbed Kyle, "Oh Kyle, I'm sorry I got a little confused."

She glanced up and found Amy too, who also had a book in hand, "Hey Mum, we were just with the librarian, she let us have a look at the books and stuff."

Emily looked up and found Bethany beside her.

"Yeah, the scary librarian was being helpful."

Emily sighed quietly, detecting an increasingly obvious tone of sarcasm.

"Here," the librarian called, "Have some breakfast.", She passed a small box which Emily just about caught. Glancing at it, she noticed it didn't specify exactly what it was, but it was military.

"What is it exactly?" she asked.

"Absolutely no idea but it is edible so, enjoy." Bethany shot Emily a look before holding her hands out, "Well go on then, go eat. Your children are fine, stop being super mum."

Emily stepped back and was greeted by the man who stopped her earlier.

"Come on, there are a few chairs down the back. I'll show you." He held out his arm and Emily did as she was instructed. As she stepped by him, she caught in a glimpse of the man's face mask, its light wasn't illuminated.

"Ermm, your mask isn't on."

The man continued walking, "Yeah, but neither is yours."

Emily slowed a little, "Really? What does that mean? Are we in danger?"

"To be honest, I don't even know why we're wearing these. What exactly is going on? Nobody knows but we're wearing them anyway."

The pair reached their destination and Emily pulled up a chair, "But if these things aren't filtering out what's bad. . ."

"Again, what are they filtering out? Right now, being de-activated, they're just thicker surgical masks, besides," the man pulled his own mask off and breathed in deeply, "You can't eat wearing one, so."

Emily put her hand to her own mask and slowly pulled it away from her ears. The black fluid, that still covered it, stuck to her skin like glue and she found herself having to tear at it to release herself from it. The man stared, taking in the face revealed under the mask.

"Looks like you've had a hell of a time out there," he held out his hand and smiled, "Name's Graham by the way."

"Emily, it's umm nice to meet you," she smiled awkwardly as she watched an embarrassed Graham retract his hand.

"Sorry, err, just seem natural to shake on meeting, but yeah, probably best." He placed the mask down and picked up the unusual military box, peeling it open, "So let's avoid the usual formalities." Emily fidgeted in her seat uncomfortably as she awaited his next question. "What the hell is going on out there? You look like you've been in a fight with some algae or something?"

Emily began to scrunch up her mask in her hands; she felt like a child, casually playing with an object before talking to someone, "Well I really don't know."

"Wow, well that's. . ." Graham paused and shook his head, "Sorry that was. . . I mean it must be as bad they say?"

"Yeah, I-we were on our way to school. Suddenly the army were all over the place and this thing - god I don't know - this thing that was somebody a moment before, and then he turned."

"Turned? Like a zombie?"

"No, no, not a zombie, but well, he became something else, his body changed. It's so hard to describe. I hit it, it ran at me and I hit it." She found herself quivering as she recalled the moment it all began, "I hit him with a metal bar, just hit him, he fell down and screamed so loudly, I don't know if it was the man or something else, but this stuff came out of him like a slime and, well, we ended up in the nearby school."

Graham shifted in his chair and found himself squeezing the box with more and more pressure.

"There were people in the school and," she recollected, "they got in, whatever they are. There were more of them." A tear trickled down her cheek as she continued, "A teacher helped us get out but something happened, they were changed."

"Like the man who you hit?"

"Yeah, but this was different, he spoke."

"Spoke?"

"It was like he was in there, but he wasn't. God it's so messed up! It called for us and it attacked. Its body, I don't know, it was so twisted and broken. We escaped and found our way into here."

"How did you, sorry I don't mean to be rude but, how did you get in here?"

Emily held up the pass she'd found. The sight of the blood-stained ID badge briefly gave Graham a lump in his throat.

"Wow, okay, you didn't umm. . . you know?"

"No! No, no, no, I wouldn't, didn't, couldn't do that, the person was dead already. We were desperate."

"It's okay, I get it, I guess whatever is out there got them too."

Emily leaned forward, "Did you know them?"

"Yeah, I mean, I worked with them, we were library staff, god this is so messed up," Graham leaned back in his chair and exhaled deeply, "So what do you think is going on?"

"I have no idea, it's insane. I mean before all this, with the restrictions, it was bad enough, now I don't even know what to think."

"Well, want to know what I think?" Graham and Emily leant towards each other, "I think it's aliens." Emily's heart sank as she closed her eyes, lowering and shaking her head. "No hear me out! A crashed space shuttle, unknown bacteria, it isn't an attack but something from beyond our world. Think of it like a virus, I don't know, a space cold!"

Emily lifted her head and shrugged her shoulders, "I guess but. . ." she raised her head further and found Janet standing beside the shelves, "Janet! Are you okay?"

"Been better," she slumped into the plastic chair and sighed," That was the most uncomfortable sleep I have ever had in my entire life." She laughed as she glanced at the pair of them, "So I take it I don't need. . .", she pointed to her mask and held her arms wide.

"Well, the light's off so I don't think it's doing much, and we're not breathing much in but dust, I hope."

Janet pulled off her mask but remained uneasy, "Are we like, sure this is. . ."

Graham smiled and patted a box behind him, "There are some fresh ones here, I say, we use them when we need to, or if we have to leave. We have enough supplies for a short while and if what your friend here says is true, we might need them."

Janet's eyes met Emily's. It was an awkward moment as Janet assumed the whole story wasn't told, but she simply nodded, glancing away from the uncomfortable mother.

"Yeah, it's hell out there. You don't have any pain killers, do you? I just have this little headache is all," Janet rubbed her head and winced as Graham stood and began rooting around in a nearby box.

"Hold on, I'll find them," Graham heroically announced, half buried in the box. Emily stood quietly and wandered down the corridor again. She felt like she had walked the same ten paces too many times already and they had only been in the shelter for a few hours.

Emily slowly paced the corridor. Shelter life was already getting to her and the need to be busy was a constant itch. There was nothing to do besides read a few thousand books. The apocalypse life was looking less and less favourable. Her children continued to play and interact with the other inhabitants of the shelter; she found herself watching as somebody would offer to show them how to draw silly animals, write a story or play simple games. Their innocence and lack fear, despite their ordeal on their way to safety, allowed her to begin to let her guard down, just a little. She set off to follow the path once again. Stopping at one of the partially open steel rollers, she found the older lady she'd encountered the night before hunched over. Her back was towards Emily.

"Excuse me? Mrs Tyson is it?" she called calmly.

The older lady looked around and caught Emily's gaze, "Oh hello, are you okay? The librarian didn't get to you, did she?"

"Oh no," Emily laughed, "She didn't, I think she's just a bit scared herself."

"Ah probably. She means well. Are you okay?"

"Yeah, I just, well. . ."

"Curiosity! You know what happened to the cat!" the old lady chuckled, and Emily's heart lifted a little, "Oh, I'm just writing. that's all."

"Writing? What are you writing?"

"Just a little diary. There's a famous book on these shelves written by somebody who kept a diary during the war and, well, it's no war but it seemed appropriate to put pen to paper. I have to be remembered for something."

"I'm sure you will make it out of here. Your family will want to see you, I'm sure."

"Well, I suppose you're right but, with all I heard you talk about on your way in, unless my knight in shining armour comes in his bulletproof vest, I'll keep my head in the pages and a pen in my hand." The older lady looked up at Emily and smiled, "Listen I think you should do the same, I'm sure people would love to hear about your heroic adventures and how you kept yourself and your children safe."

Emily shifted uncomfortably and shook her head, "No, I doubt anyone will want to hear how I crumbled under pressure."

"Nonsense, I won't have it. Here take these and sit down. I insist," the older lady held out a library branded pen and a black notebook, pushing past her to drag the metal chair across the floor, "Now come on, sit. I want to see some words on that paper."

Emily slumped into the chair besides the older lady who signalled for her to get on with it. She felt uncomfortable and completely out of her depth. She clicked the pen and began to rock it in her hand. Beside her, the older woman wrote furiously and with such confidence. Emily wished she could do likewise. She stared at the paper and breathed in, giving herself an internal pep talk and then beginning to write, it was like being ten years old again.

Dear diary. This sucks.

Emily closed her eyes and shook her head; she knew she was acting like a sulky teenager. It was hard to put anything on paper that she felt would be interesting or relevant to whoever may read it in the future, if there was a future for them. As she sat quietly talking to herself, she could hear the excited laughter of her children, that gave her motivation. She needed to let them know how she felt, why she wanted to protect them. She couldn't let them forget the hardships they were bound to endure. Emily clicked the pen twice, as if it were a starting gun, and steadily began to write.

My name is Emily Farragher. This is not something I have ever done but, maybe one day, my children or someone else will read this and understand just what we've all been through. I mean, what are we facing? I've not had a moment to stop yet, it's been maybe 24 hours since it all began. Maybe I should talk about that?

Emily rested the pen against the paper and looked up at her companion who continued to write, words covered her page from top to bottom.

A lovely lady got me to write this. I didn't understand why at first but it's more than just venting to a piece of paper. It's about remembering who we are, telling our story to those who may never know me. God that's depressing but, should something happen, I hope, whatever drama I write down, my family will know I love them. I'm apart from the love of my life right now and his support would go a long way in helping me make sense of this chaos. I hope you're safe Jack.

Emily closed the diary and clicked the pen down.

"Hey, umm, thanks for this."

The older lady turned around and smiled, "Oh, it's okay, just something to keep us out of mischief, aye?" Emily wandered out from between the steel rollers, diary in hand, smiling to herself. For once she felt alright, it was nice to take her mind off things and stop, it might be far from normal, but she was in good company. Safe hands. As she stepped back into the corridor, Emily bumped into the librarian.

"Oh, I'm sorry!" she called out.

"No, no, it's me," Bethany awkwardly brushed her arm

before leaning casually against the wall, "I was looking for you actually."

Emily waited expecting to receive another rant, "Oh me? How come?"

"I actually wanted to apologise for last night."

Emily's wide-eyed reaction gave her away.

"I mean, I don't think I should have shouted, you know?" Bethany squirmed a little like a child owning up to breaking mum's favourite cup.

"Hey, it's okay. I'd be erratic too if someone had invaded my shelter in the middle of the night covered in god knows what and holding an, ermm, ID card," Emily paused and regretted bringing the ID card up again, "I'm sorry I. . ."

"No, it's okay, I was just a bit on edge, you know? I mean I don't really think you killed her!" Bethany laughed awkwardly as Emily avoided looking at her, "Anyway, I'm sorry, okay. Your kids seem pretty nice though."

Emily peered past the librarian and saw her children calmly drawing on the corridor floor, "Yeah, they are. Thanks for distracting them, I appreciate it. They've already been through a lot and I think, with everyone down here, it's taken their Dad off their minds."

"Oh, is he. . ."

"Dead? No. We were on our way into school We left their Dad, Jack, at home. He was supposed to be finishing our home shelter," she paused and leaned against the wall, "Shit, I hope he's okay. We just left him; I gave him a kiss and. . . that might be it." Bethany watched as a tear ran down Emily's cheek.

"Hey, listen. I'm sure he's fine, swigging a coffee in safety, probably worried about you! Would he have a phone with him?" she slipped a smartphone from her pocket and waved it a little,

"Here, use mine if you think he will answer."

Emily rubbed her sleeve across her eyes. She nodded and mouthed a thank you as she took the phone from Bethany's hand. She shook a little as she tapped in Jack's number and hit the call button. Placing the phone to her ear she closed her eyes and lifted her head to the sky almost praying in between each ring. Eventually the ringing stopped, Emily twisted on the spot.

"Jack?" she almost screamed down the phone, "Jack can you hear me?"

"Hey, it's Jack. . . leave a message after the beep."

Emily sank to the floor, desperately trying to control her emotions. "Jack. . . please call me back, I need to hear you. . . I need to know you're safe. Please." Emily hit the end call button and rose, placing the phone back into the librarian's hands, and slowly slunk down the corridor. She clenched her fists as she wandered through, unaware of the looks everyone gave her; she didn't care, she was so angry, so emotional, completely lost, wanting to have her family together, wanting something to give her the hope she needed. She reached her children who were still sitting on the floor drawing. Kyle turned, pencil in hand and marker pen across his cheek,

"Hey mum look I drew a. . ." Before Kyle could show his mother his impressive artwork, he found himself completely swamped by her warm body, his mother's tears trickling down his own face as she embraced him hard.

"I love you," she whispered, struggling to pull in Amy who defiantly tugged away, although she would soon join in.

"Mum, come on," Amy sighed, embarrassed, but in a loving way, "We're going to be okay."

Emily hoped that would be true and closed her eyes tighter, enjoying the moment.

Chapter 5

Emily lay on her back. She stared at the dull green glow from the emergency light, almost mesmerised, she prayed she might just distract herself long enough to sleep, but it was not to be. Her attempted call to her husband made her face reality, the shelter wasn't providing what she wanted. Yes, it was safe, and they weren't in immediate danger, but she wanted her family to be together. As she lay on the cold, hard concrete floor, her children wrapped in her arms, she noticed that the bay beside her, that provided the sleeping quarters for the teacher they had joined up with, was shaking. Emily released her daughter from her arms and used her free hand to move a cardboard box across the shelf to give her a view of the next-door space. She froze in horror as she stared at Janet, who was shivering and breathing erratically.

"Janet are you alright?" she stammered.

Janet slowly met Emily's wide-eyed gaze but didn't utter a word as she began to squirm restlessly. Emily closed her eyes; this could not be happening; Janet couldn't be infected! Looking over again, she watched as Janet began to curl up in agony. Emily quickly roused her children who awoke with a shock.

"We need to move now!" she whispered as she frantically

pushed them to their feet.

"Mum what's wrong?" Amy asked rubbing her eyes. As she did so, she twisted and caught a glimpse of her teacher writhing in pain, "Mum!"

"Get over to the wall now, don't look, just move," Emily lurched forward and pushed her children against the corridor wall, "Do not move!"

As she tried to step away Kyle grabbed her hand, "Where are you. . ?"

"Just wait here, I'm getting something." Emily wrestled her hand away from her terrified son and headed for the back wall where the supply boxes were stacked high, covering the steel shelves. She began to peel them open, being carefully not to make any sound to alert the others. She knew, if anyone should wake now, they would blame her for bringing an infected person inside the shelter. She was terrified of what they might do. After searching through a few boxes, she finally came across a plain black backpack and immediately started to fill it with supplies of food, bottled water, spare masks - anything they might need to deal with whatever was to happen next. As she finished packing, she found Bethany standing in front of her.

"What the hell are you doing?"

Emily felt like a child caught stealing from the biscuit tin. She had nothing to say, and this just infuriated the librarian further.

"Are you stealing?" As Bethany stepped towards Emily, a deafening scream filled the air. Looking down the corridor, Emily saw her children sprinting towards them.

"Mum! Miss is sick, she's screaming on the floor!" Amy shouted, the fear in her voice plain to hear. Emily gripped the backpack tighter as Bethany turned to face her again.

"You fucking bitch, you knew she was infected!" Bethany

shoved the paralysed mother almost onto her back, luckily the stack of supply boxes broke her fall. "Are you infected too?" Bethany clenched her fist ready to throw a punch as Janet screamed loudly again.

Emily noticed a door to her right. Bolting from the wall, she grabbed the handle and swung it open.

"Kids, now, move!" Emily stood aside as the children darted through the doorway and into the room beyond, its emergency lighting only just providing enough illumination to see by. As Emily tried to follow them, Bethany grabbed her shirt and pulled her back.

"I don't think so, bitch!"

Emily was winded as she fell onto her back. She lay, trying to catch her breathe. Bethany stood over her, as she raised her fist again, another pair of arms grabbed the librarian's.

"What are you do. . ?" Graham tried to pull the librarian away but found himself wrapped in, what looked like, an octopus' tentacle. The tall man dropped to the floor and was quickly dragged away from the feuding women, his face scraping across the concrete. Janet stood at an angle, the left side of her body almost double its original size, the new tentacle-like arm retracting back inside it, the sound popping rapidly as the monster stumbled from the shelving. Bethany stepped back, trying desperately to find the taser she'd threatened Emily with when they'd first met, but there was nothing but fabric to grab at. Her eyes wide with fear, Bethany backed away, but it was too late. The monster Janet had become screamed again, lashing out, using her arm as a weapon she hit out at Bethany who fell, hitting the floor hard before being dragged away with extreme speed. Seizing her moment, Emily threw herself forward, frantically grabbed the backpack and scrabbled for the door. Almost shoulder barging her way in, Emily stumbled inside, slamming the door behind her. She stepped into the darkness and found her children huddled on the floor.

"It's okay, shhh." Emily grabbed them both tightly, the screams of the shelter survivors echoing loudly around the room. "Follow me. Hold my bag, Amy. Kyle, don't let go of your sister, do you understand?" But Kyle couldn't do as he'd been told, immobile from fear as the sounds of the vicious attack reverberated around him. He knew what lay out there and simply refused to move. Emily reached the door, turning the handle, but Amy couldn't feel her brother's hand and pulled on her mother's backpack.

"Mum, where's Kyle?" The pair of them desperately tried to peer through the darkness. Suddenly, they were bathed in light as the monster smashed away a large chunk of the door with its incredibly powerful tentacle arm, letting out a deafening screamed. The pair stumbled back inside the room to find Kyle. The light through the hole in the broken door revealed where he sat. Emily ran to her son and simply picked him up. She turned to find Amy close by as the monster continued to destroy the door in its attempt to reach them.

"Hold on Amy", she instructed. Amy grabbed her once more as Emily reached for the door and opened it, stumbling over the debris created by the monster's fight with the shelves. The three of them fought their way down the corridor, for what they knew would be their last time. As Emily moved hastily, she couldn't help but stop as she noticed the old lady who had given her the diary, the desire to write her story. She found herself simply staring, the lady had tears running down her face but nodded at her and, with a wave of her hand, ushered to her to go. Emily obliged, moving steadily forward. As she reached the door, she spotted the librarian's taser laid carefully on a pile of books.

"Kyle, you need to listen, okay? We're going to run. I need you to do that, okay?"

Kyle nodded furiously before waving his hand forward and shouting, "Mum look out!" As Emily spun around, Kyle's hand was pointing beyond her and Emily came face to face with a battered and bloodied librarian who stood, seething with rage. As she exhaled, a fine spray of blood came from her mouth. Emily raised the taser and held it against the other woman's chest. Bethany pushed against it like it was a challenge.

"Bethany, I'm sorry, I am really, but I have to get out of her, for their sakes." Emily crept back a little as the librarian continued to lean towards her, "Seriously, I will shoot you! Stop!" As the librarian continued to move forward, the stand-off was interrupted by the monster who had battered the door into the shelter with such force that the wood exploded around the room like a grenade. The four of them dropped to the floor. Emily scrambled to support herself, she found Amy shouting in her face, but she couldn't hear any more than a mumble. She watched as her daughter tried desperately to talk to her, but it seemed that nothing was coming out of her mouth. Emily turned away and the world swiftly came back into focus as the monster furiously slammed the librarian into the room. With the monster distracted, she tried to pull herself up, but her body her legs gave way and she found herself stumbling instead. Her children had managed to reach the stairs they had used to enter the shelter and were shouting to her.

"Mum, come on please, we can get out here!" Amy screamed as she pointed to a door labelled 'Fire Exit'. She was poised and ready to push the silver bar. Emily grabbed the taser and pushed it into her jean's pocket, hobbling to the door she didn't stop this time. There was nothing more she could do, she had to move. With determined steps she pulled herself up the stairs and waved to her daughter standing at the door.

"Do it, push it now!" she gasped in pain. As she called out, Amy pushed the bar and, with a very satisfying click, the world was revealed again to them, albeit in the dark of night-time. The children stepped out quickly and Amy pulled her mother from the stairway.

"Kyle, push that door closed!" she called over her shoulder as she guided her mother to an adjacent wall. Collapsing against it. Emily breathed heavily and looked up at her daughter who had pulled Kyle from the door back towards them.

"Hey, that was brave," Emily smiled although the pain glanced through her own battered body. "Let's try not to make this a habit though, okay?" she laughed and grimaced at the same time. Kyle got up close to his mother and hugged her. She tensed as she tried to resist asking him not to squeeze so hard, "It's okay Kyle, we're out, we're okay."

Amy stood over her mother and stared at the bloodied shirt that was beginning to cling to her chest.

"Mum, are you okay?" Silly question she thought, but it was an instinct.

"Yeah, I think." Emily tried to move but found her body tensing in agony. "On second thoughts, I'll just sit here a little longer." She slowly moved her arm, grabbed the bottom of her top and pulled carefully upward. As she pulled, the blood from her wounds dripped down her body. Flakes of debris crumbled off her shirt, but some remained neatly arranged across her stomach. Amy leaned down and gave her mum a look.

"You're not okay Mum, look at you!"

"Okay, yeah, I guess not," Emily sighed as her body started to relax, "But we can't stay here, can we?"

"Where can we go, though? Those things are everywhere, they're going to kill us!"

"We're a few streets from home, we should see if your dad is okay." Emily carefully lifted her head, "If you can both pull me up, we can go home, your dad can help me then."

The children's faces lit up at the thought of finally seeing their father again. They each grabbed one of their mother's hands, "Okay kids. . . Pull!" She bit on her tongue tightly as pain surged through her, miraculously she was lifted back onto her feet. "Right get either side of me, we're going home. Amy grab that backpack, we're going to need it." Emily nodded in the direction of the backpack she had stolen from the library. Amy slowly let go of her mother and pulled the backpack on. Slipping back under their mother's arms, the three of them hobbled towards the dimly lit streets.

Making their way out of the back street, they found themselves emerging back into the chaos that appeared before them. Cars were left abandoned, their doors flung open, not by any monsters, but in an attempt by their owners to run rather than risk driving off. Litter and debris blew gently around, covering the dead that lay on the streets. Emily stepped back a little and glanced at her children, who barely spoke or moved.

"Okay, eyes up! Just think we are so close to home, just that street. . . one street. Come on, we can do it. Just think, Dad will have all that bunker to himself. He'll probably even have eaten all those tasty snacks you put in there, Kyle." At her urging, her children very tentatively crept forward, "Okay, slow and steady then." As they moved cautiously into the dim yellow light and onto the main street, a group stepped out and made their presence known.

"Hey guys, what are you doing out here all alone?" the lead man asked with a curious look.

"We're just getting out of here," Emily groaned as she pulled on her children who edged closer together, "We live just behind that building there."

"Oh, but it looks like you have too much to carry. Why don't we take that off you?" The man stepped forward displaying a disturbing smile.

"Listen we don't want any trouble; we just want to get off this street."

"Oh, come on, we insist," the man turned to the others and waved his hand; the group began to move slowly towards them.

"No, come on, we have nothing to give you, it's just an empty pack!" Emily pulled her children back, limping as she tried to move away. The group laughed amongst themselves and pressed on slowly. Amy glanced back, trying not to fall over as she sought to avoid the debris that covered the street. As she stepped back, she noticed the taser jammed into her mother's pocket and, without hesitation, removed her mother's arm from her shoulder and pulled hard, releasing the taser.

"Get back!" she stood with the taser pointing at the lead man, who stopped for a moment before laughing.

"What? Get that toy out of my face!" The man lurched towards Amy who, in her panic, pulled the trigger and released the dart from the taser. The man's crude smile changed quickly as electricity surged through the thin wire and was fired into his body. He collapsed, twitching on the ground. Amy stood wide eyed, loosening the taser from her grip and standing motionless.

"Jesus Amy, what did you do?" Emily pulled Amy back in and

grabbed her as the group of men stood shell-shocked before grunting and moving closer again. As the men moved quickly, Emily felt an overwhelming pain in her stomach. Letting go of Kyle, she clutched at her body in agony, screaming as she dropped to her side.

"Mum! Mum, please get up, please!" Amy screamed at her mother, who was screaming even louder. Amy looked over her shoulder, the men were right on top of them now, "Mum please!" As Amy screamed louder, Emily's eyes opened wide, and she shuddered before vomiting huge amounts of black bile. The men shouted to each other before running off down the street and leaving the family alone. Amy jumped back and pulled Kyle violently by his collar to move him away from their mother.

"Mum, what the hell is happening?"

Emily panted for a moment and looked up at her children. They stared back in disbelief as she surged forward, mumbling incoherently as she tried to speak. The bile continued to run from her mouth to cover the front of her body. The children dived to either side and stepped behind her, tears running down their cheeks, as they watched their mother scream again and drop to her knees as she forced out one word, "Run!"

Without hesitation, Amy grabbed her little brother's hand and made a run for it. Emily watched as her children fled from her in fear, knowing what would come next. Her visioned blackened and she dropped to the floor.

Chapter 6

Amy barely managed to put one foot in front of the other as she dragged her brother close behind her, her hand tightly squeezing his as they made a run for it into the town centre. She glanced behind and, with the coast clear, swung to her left, sliding on the rubble and pulling Kyle down to the floor.

"Stop, stop!" she whispered, feeling an ache in her throat, "Stay here." Amy slowly got onto her knees and shuffled to the corner, carefully peering around it. She stared intensely down the long, wide road lit up by various shop signs, "Okay, I think we're okay."

"But what about Mum?" Kyle tugged on Amy's jacket, "What about Mum?"

"She's one of them now!" Amy shouted, "She's gone, it's just us!"

"No, Mum's okay, she has to be!"

"Did you see what she did? The others all did that sick thing and then they became whatever they are!"

"No!" Kyle shouted as he started to hit out at his sister, "No, I want Mum!"

"Listen!" Amy grabbed Kyle and pulled him tight to her chest, wrapping her arms around him, "Mum's gone. I'm sorry," she stuttered a little as she spoke, hardly able to believe what she was saying. Kyle sobbed into her jacket and Amy found herself frozen in place, she couldn't think, all that ran through her head was, "What would mum do?"

As she closed her eyes and squeezed her brother tighter, the sound of something breaking brought her back into the moment. She peeled Kyle from her and held her finger to her lips before swinging round to see the street again. Slowly dragging its body across the floor, a monster made its move up the street, drawing a disgusting, pulsing sack behind it. Amy shuffled back and pulled Kyle up from the floor.

"Move now, come on. one of those things is coming!"

"Is it mum?" Kyle looked into Amy's eyes and she stood for a moment wondering if it could actually be her mother.

"I don't know, I can't see its face. Come on, we shouldn't see her like that if it is." Amy took Kyle's hand and escorted her younger brother into the town centre. The children moved carefully up the street, dodging the debris, side-stepping the bodies strewn along it and carefully avoiding any contact with anyone else after learning very quickly that everybody had lost it. All that Amy wanted to do was to protect Kyle and to stay safe. She couldn't trust anyone; it was the two of them and that was it. What were they supposed to do? Where should they go? As she tried to think what to do next, she felt Kyle tug on her arm.

"Amy, I'm tired. Can we stop?"

Amy looked at the little boy's face; it was covered in dust and he was obviously exhausted, "We can't, not yet. We have to keep going till we know we're safe."

"Amy, please! I'm so tired," He pulled his hand out of her grasp and folded his arms, "You're not Mum anyway." With that he turned to face the shop window.

"No, I'm not, but I know she would say keep going and it'll be okay. Come on, we can stop soon." Amy tried to grab Kyle who shuffled just out of reach. "No, come on please." Kyle grunted again and Amy stepped up to him, turning to face the window too. Inside the shop, items were scattered - newspapers, magazines, just about everything was thrown on the floor.

Amy smiled, "Alright, I'm not mum but that's good." She picked her way over the broken glass in the doorway and nodded at Kyle to go inside, "Want to try fizzy pop?"

Kyle turned towards her with a grin on his face, "Yeah!" The pair stepped inside and giggling as they began to pocket various chocolates and sweets from the shelves. Kyle, his face lit up with excitement, reached into the fridge for a bottle of, what he knew, was fizzy pop, something his Dad had bought before.

"Amy, can I try this one?" Kyle held the bottle towards her and smiled as he handed it over.

"Alright. Now this is called Cola; enjoy it, it'll wake you up at least!" She unscrewed the lid and Kyle chuckled as the bottle gave out a gentle click and hissed in her hands. He grabbed the bottle, quickly removed his mask, and started to drink. He gulped it down hard; the fizz liquid filling the bottle spilled over the top, catching him by surprise. He slowly raised his head to look at his sister who covered her mouth with her hands trying desperately not to laugh out loud. Kyle took another swig of the fizzy drink, laughing loudly as it dribbled down his chin onto the floor. Amy stepped forward and swung the backpack around.

"Come on, grab some things, we can fill it for later." Amy pointed to the fridge before stepping to the shelf beside it and starting to pick up sweets, chocolate bars, crisps, all the nice but unhealthy treats that Mum and Dad often only gave them in small quantities; something about losing all their teeth would always come up in the conversation. The children giggled as they crammed the backpack with their new treats.

"Okay I think this will be enough," Amy grunted as she zipped up the backpack and swung it onto her back, "Oh wow, this is heavy."

"I got loads!" Kyle grinned as he stood rubbing his little hands together. Amy smiled and stepped up to her brother, leaning down on one knee and placing his mask back across his face.

"I saw. Remember to put this back on, okay, Mum wouldn't be happy."

"I know, I'm sorry," Kyle leaned to the side and rocked his foot a little.

"Hey, it's okay Kyle," Amy tried to comfort him, but a grotesque rapping sound caught her attention. She frantically pulled her mask back across her face, twisting as she held her arm out to push Kyle behind her, "Kyle stay behind me. Hey, who's there?" she quivered.

"Thaaat's fiiive. . .niinety. . .nineeee," a harsh and grizzled voice came from behind the shop counter.

"I didn't mean to steal, we were, my brother we. . ," Amy continued to step back whilst trying to peer into the darkness to see what she was confronting.

"Steeeealing. . ." the voice hissed, the body behind it rising with a crunching sound as it revealed itself. Amy screamed on seeing its distorted, torn body, its face barely recognisable, its twisted neck trying to find a way to turn its head to see the children.

"Kyle, run!" Amy turned and pushed Kyle out of the shop, almost onto the floor, as he tried to meet his sister's demands,

"Come on, move!" As they stepped out on to the pavement, Amy spun round momentarily trying to think about which way to go. Her answer came in the form of the monster smashing through the window, screaming as it lunged its already torn body through the glass, the disgusting black and green liquid from its wounds oozing beneath it. Amy stumbled backwards almost knocking Kyle over before grabbed her brother's hand.

"Run!" The pair moved as fast as they could. The monster screamed and gave chase, slamming its distorted body against everything in its path as it battered its way towards them. Amy moved as fast as she could but found it hard with Kyle straggling behind her.

"Kyle, come on, move!" Amy shouted as Kyle panted from trying to match his sister's pace. In his haste, Kyle tripped and fell to the ground, scraping his hands across the floor. He lay on his front, completely frozen in fear. His eyes widened as he heard the loud footsteps of the monster following them. Amy stumbled forward, twisting to face her brother.

"Kyle!" she screamed running back to him with her hands outstretched to protect her brother. The monster twisted its arm from which a large ball of flesh emerged, forming itself into a fist and slamming into Amy who flew sideways into the shop beside her. She found herself winded, lying in a pile of toys and metal shelving. Amy rolled on her back in agony, her body had never been in such pain, her every sense in complete shock as she attempted to come to. As her entire body adjusted to the situation, the monster's shadow grew larger. Amy found herself wide eyed as the monster screamed, lifting its gigantic fist into the air, and breaking the fragile roof panels as it prepared to strike. Amy rolled and scrambled off the floor as the fist smashed into the ground, levelling the shelving, and creating a large dent in the store's flooring. She stumbled through, glancing over her shoulder repeatedly as she tried to stay a step ahead. The monster used its large body to barge the shelves aside as it moved forward. Amy side-stepped through the closing gap and fumbled against the wall as the shelves moved like a wave. Trapped, she began to panic and frantically looked around for anything she might be able to use to defend herself. She found her weapon as she brushed up against the shop's fire extinguisher. Amy lifted then quickly dropped it. Pushing it in front of her, she pulled the hose and pulled the trigger. Nothing! Amy tugged on the trigger as the monster continued to batter the metal shelves away like they were twigs. Eventually, the coloured tag broke and the extinguisher squirmed in her hands as the compressed gas screamed from the red canister, creating a wall of fog between her and the monster.

Suddenly, everything went quiet. Amy stood, breathing heavily, and coughing from the extinguisher fog fumes. In the mist, the monster reached out and grabbed the canister, popping it like a balloon. The monster squirmed forward, twisting around before splitting in two and revealing a dark-coloured skeleton as it swayed from side to side before dropping to the floor. Amy jumped back as the monster began to dissolve around her and scrambled on to the metal shelving that provided an island for her. The smell was nauseating. She tried desperately not to throw up. She had no idea what she was breathing in and didn't want to become as deformed as the monsters she had encountered recently. She darted across the tops of the shelving and made a break for the front of the shop, attempting to make her way back to Kyle. Though still in pain, she clattered over the shelving and slid off the end. As she reached the door she steadily slowed.

"Kyle? Are you okay?" she called calmly, "Kyle, come on, come here." Her brother hesitantly shuffled to the side and made his way towards his sister. In front of them stood a man, head to toe in black, with a backpack of his own, he held his hands up to signal his intentions.

"Hey, it's okay. I heard the shouting and just wanted to see what was going on," the man peered behind Amy and pointed at the fallen monster, "Wow, did you do that?"

Amy nodded as she pushed Kyle behind her, "I did."

"Wow, that's impressive." The man stepped forwards slowly, the children stepped back, "Hey it's cool, I'm just making sure you guys are okay."

"We're fine," Amy bluntly replied still shielding Kyle, "We just want to get out of here."

"Well, that's understandable. Hey, is it just you two?" the man asked lowering his hands. Amy nodded. "Oh, where's Mum or Dad? Are you guys out here all alone?"

"Our parents are nearby, you sho-"

"Our Mum turned," Kyle spoke quietly as he leaned from behind his sister.

"Oh no, I am so sorry, that must have been scary."

Kyle nodded as Amy stepped in front of him and stared hard, "But our Dad is out there, I think. Some men attacked us on our way home. We're just looking to hide."

"Well, that's fair enough. Why don't you come with me? I'm from a safehouse a little out of the way." The man leaned down and pointed to the emblem on his arm, "Do you know what this is?" The children shook their heads. "It's the trust symbol. I work at the Abbey on the outskirts of town, I bet you know it?" They nodded in unison. "Perfect, well if you'll let me, I can take you to my safehouse. We have power and phones. Maybe we can contact your Dad?" Kyle's eyes lit up and he shuffled to Amy's side, pulling at her arm, and nodding quickly. Amy leaned on Kyle and pushed him back.

"We'll follow you. But I do have a weapon," Amy made a gun shape in her jacket, "I got this taser from someone and I can use it."

The man laughed and held his hands high as he stepped back, "Hey, that's a safe thing, gotta be safe, yeah? Come on, I'll lead. Stay close, okay, it's dark up this way." Amy held her brother's hand tightly and the pair of them followed the helpful man out into the debris-covered town centre to begin their long trip into the darkness ahead of them.

Chapter 7

In the dimly lit street where she had blacked out, Emily slowly awoke. Her body felt strange, it was as if she had been on an all-night wine binge. As she lay there, her mind felt separate from her body. She carefully attempted to move but found she could only twitch slightly as the pain caused by her face resting on the broken tarmac flowed through her body. In a panic, her eyes widened, and she tried to scream. Nothing but a muffled sound followed, she was almost paralysed, and fear was setting in. Repeatedly, she tried to push her body to move - her head, her waist, her hands, her fingers, down through her legs to her toes - in a cycle, over and over. Gradually, her body began to react, and she found herself on her hands and knees. Just as she began to feel a sense of success, a sharp pain coursed through her body causing a thumping at the front of her head; it did not let up. Emily screamed as she collapsed again. As she became more alarmed, her breathing became erratic. Opening her eyes, the world began to twist and change; it turned dark, the light a peculiar shade of green.

Eventually, her pain eased, leaving her relieved. Twisting, she knelt on the ground. Emily peered around at the recognisable, yet different, world. She experienced an unnerving sensation as she felt something tunnelling and moving through her. She flipped over, rubbing her eyes, scrabbling around on the floor in sheer confusion. It stopped suddenly. The world seemed to move in slow motion, dull sounds echoed around her.

"Hello?" she called out into the darkness, "Hello, please I need help." She slid herself over to a wall and slumped against it, the intense drunk feeling taking her over once again as she fought the almost overwhelming urge to vomit. She closed her eyes in an attempt to stop the world from spinning and counted slowly to ten.

"One, two, three, four, five, six, seven, eight, nine, ten. . ." She lifted her head; the world still moved freely whilst she didn't. It had become even more grotesque; strange plant-like vines covered the street walls and flowed freely onto the pavement. She felt sick as she wondered where her children had gone. Her mind was filled with a flurry of questions and her head ached.

"Kyle! Amy!" she shouted, her voice toneless and dull as she repeated the call. "Kids!" She recalled the moment before she had passed out, more questions and thoughts filling her head. "Oh no, no, no. Kids, please!" She pushed herself up using the wall behind her as a support and stumbled into the street, "Kids, please. . . I'm not sick, I'm not. . ." she cried out.

Standing in the middle of the street to get her bearings, a strange noise almost echoed back to her in reply.

"Hello?" she called out cautiously into the darkness. The noise became a snakelike hiss coming towards her. Emily spun round to catch its origin. In the distance a shadowy figure stood; it was unmoving and only just discernible in the unusual, green-tinted light. She staggered towards the shadow, "Hello? Please I need some help." The figure remained motionless as she stumbled on, clutching the wall for balance. "Please, I'm not sick, I promise." She remembered the bile she had vomited before she'd blacked out and the realisation that she just might actually really be sick hit her hard. She fell backwards, scrapping her arm against the sharp pebble-dashing of the wall. Holding her arm up to inspect it, a shadow in the distance caught her attention. It rose up to reveal a long wire which seemed to tether it to the ground. Emily stared as it lifted before splitting in two, shaking violently. In fear, Emily could barely move as she watched the dark shape twist; the sound of tearing flesh hit her like surround sound and, in that moment, she turned and ran. A dark, morbid scream filled the streets. Emily faltered on, using anything she could find to support her body and keep her upright.

She dared not look back and continued to move forwards. The sounds of the ground cracking and metal scraping filled her ears as the monster moved, like a tank, through whatever stood in its path. Emily desperately pulled her heavy body across the street, bumping carelessly into the abandoned cars that littered the main road, before finding herself on the floor. She quickly forced her back to the car door and closed her eyes, hoping for the monster to move on without noticing her. She counted to herself again to control her breathing, trying to find the courage to make a break for it. Emily slowly twisted around the battered car. The monster was almost on top of her now. She stumbled away from the car, scrabbling on the floor to get away.

"No, no, no!" she called out as she slipped on her own weak hands. As she lay there, the monster steadily moved towards her. The world kept slipping away, and any words she managed to get out went unheard, as her eyes closed and she lost consciousness.

Chapter 8

Emily groaned as she slowly came to; her head ached but it was nothing like the horrendous sharp pain that had shot through it only moments ago. The realisation that she was alive, upright and lying against a car filled her with immediate panic. The adrenaline lifted her as she pushed against the floor. Slipping against the car bonnet, she came face to face with a tall, scruffy, dark haired man who looked just as startled as she did.

"Who are you?" she shouted nearly tripping over the car for a third time.

"Shhh!" the man covered her mouth. Emily grabbed the man's hand and began to pull it away. "Stop shouting, there's one of them nearby." Emily stopped struggling as the distant scream from one of the many monsters inhabiting the town filled the air. As the man became distracted by the noise, she managed to push his hand from her face.

"Alright, I get it, but, Jesus, could you not have just told me?"

"Well, you've spent the last five minutes running from me. You didn't exactly give me much choice."

Emily thought for a moment, "What do you mean running from you? There was a monster, and I was avoiding it."

The man shook his head and pointed to himself, "Honestly do I look messed up with weird shit hanging off me?" He ran his hands up and down his body, his eyes wide, "Come on, I was calling out to you." He stepped to the side and grabbed a backpack, pulling it on. "I was trying to see if you were alright. Clearly you are," the man spoke with a sarcastic tone.

"Okay, okay, I'm sorry. Thank you, I appreciate the thought but I'm trying to find my children."

The man raised an eyebrow, "You've lost your own children?"

Emily glared at him as he raised his hands. "Of course not, we were attacked by some idiots who tried to rob us. I passed out," she paused for a moment as she recalled the scene like a nightmare running through her head. She glanced back to the man and decided it would be best not to tell the whole truth, "We were in the library when someone turned, we barely got out," she moved her shirt to reveal the scars, "I think the adrenaline ran out on me."

"Your kids must have been scared to have left you."

Emily paused again as she recalled her children's panic-stricken faces, "Yeah, I bet."

"I'm on a supply run and, well, I think I have enough. Maybe you should come back to my shelter with me."

"Your shelter?" Emily asked puzzled.

"Well, not mine but I help look after it, it's the old Abbey. There's an underground section that was being dug up for public viewing, we're using that to stay hidden. It's a bit of a maze to be honest," the man laughed a little and cleared his throat, "There was someone else with me. If he's found your kids, maybe he's taken them back to give them shelter as well."

Emily met the man's gaze and nodded reluctantly. She didn't know the man or trust him, but what other options did she really have at this point? She needed something to treat the cuts from the beating she'd received and could do with food and water.

"Okay, fine, but I need your name first. I don't even know you."

The man laughed and held out his hand, "Oh, absolutely! Name's John." She glanced at the hand but given her 'condition', didn't think it would be wise to shake it. John paused and pointed down the centre of the shopping area, "I'll lead, yeah? It's a bit of a trek but we're planning for the long term and nowhere nearby really had much. Here, have some water on me." John twisted the bag off his back and unzipped it, producing a plastic bottle of water, and handing it to her. Emily grabbed it like a child receiving a cake and drank it at once. Her throat ached from whatever had escaped her body earlier. Emily sighed as she let the bottle drop to her side and put her thumbs up. In the awkward silence she ushered him to take the lead.

"Oh sorry, yeah, follow me." John fumbled with the zip and pulled the bag back over himself, leading Emily back through the quiet and litter-strewn town centre.

As they walked, not much was said at first. The constant threat of attack and noises in the distance echoing around them meant that they spent most of the first leg of their journey nipping behind walls before sneaking through shops and alleyways to avoid contact with whatever was out there. Emily had seen first-hand what other survivors were willing to do, and clearly her new friend, John, had too, though he had taken a moment to help her. She didn't know what to make of him yet but the opportunity to find her children was top priority.

After a short while the pair made it out of the town centre and onto the main road. Emily turned to look along it, the library standing out not far away. She couldn't help but feel all kinds of emotions as she thought about those she'd left in the shelter below, perhaps as well, how little progress she had really made in getting anywhere in the meantime. In the space of nearly three, maybe four, days, who knew, she had gone from her home, to the school, over to the library and was back on the streets again; it had been relentless. Now she hobbled along with a man she didn't know, following streets she barely recognised, wondering less about if her husband was alive and more hoping that he didn't suffer. Emily paused at the corner of the road as John briskly wandered on. She glanced down a side-street leading off the large main road and imagined the route she often took from the main town centre. It would be so easy to get back home from here, but would the outcome be worth it?

"John, do you have a phone?" John swivelled and shrugged.

"Really? A phone? Now?"

"Yes, just answer me. Yes or no?"

"No, I don't. Now come on, please. We aren't safe at all," John huffed and strode away. Emily turned and steadily picked up her pace to catch up. They moved carefully, keeping in the shadows as much as possible and using the main road's intense treeline to their advantage; ensuring any monsters, or aggressive survivors, wouldn't spot them in the morning light that was ever so slowly creeping over the horizon. Every building they wandered past was littered with broken glass. Emily tried hard to avoid looking in and walked as quickly as she could, but every so often a glimpse of a broken body, inside a half-lit shop, would catch her eye. Trails of black ooze creeping in and around the buildings gathered in the streets like a river.

The cover provided by the buildings stopped as they reached the railway line that had once provided travel to and from the town. Strangely, two trains sat there, their lights dim but enough to light the way. Emily hovered, staring down to the station.

"John, what's going on?" she waved her finger at the station, "Is someone down there?"

John stepped back and looked towards where Emily was pointing.

"No, well, bodies but not people. I guess they got caught out. I don't know. Come on, we should keep moving, we're barely halfway there." John tried to hold Emily's shoulder but found himself stumbling forward as she leaned away from him.

"Listen, if there's any. . ."

"There isn't, I went down to see myself. They're dead, okay?"

Emily took another glance, shaking her head before continuing to walk down the street. John quickly stepped up to her and tried hard to keep ahead as she aggressively held the pace. The pair reached the gates of the town's local park. John turned to face Emily.

"Okay, so if we follow this road, it gets pretty quiet from here on." As John tried to reassure Emily, a loud crash filled the air and caught both of them off guard. The pair moved to take cover behind the large park gates' brick barrier and stood immobile. Behind them on the street. another monster stood proudly and territorially on top of a car, its body twisted and animal-like. Emily only caught a glimpse of the monster, but it was enough for her to know that she wasn't getting back on to those streets.

"John, what now?" she whispered.

"We need to go through the park, follow the path to the opposite exit." John leaned back quickly as the monster's voice rumbled around the open space. It jumped to the ground, moving like a dog sniffing out its prey, "Move, now!" John moved cautiously away from the wall and began to walk briskly, waving his hand to usher Emily to follow. The pair kept low as they climbed the hill, the dawning sunrise lighting their way. The monument at the top acted as their next checkpoint. As John began to jog, Emily slowed, her body aching intensely as she pushed her upper body and legs hard. She held her hand to her chest, feeling the blood seeping back through her shirt again.

"John please," she stopped and collapsed to her knees.

"Emily, are you okay?" John swivelled and knelt beside her, "Hey, come on. It's not far now."

"You keep saying that," Emily winced, "But I feel like I'm going nowhere. Honestly, I'm wondering what I'm doing."

John moved to Emily's side and lifted her free arm over his shoulder.

"What you're doing is going to see your children. Now quit talking and hold on." John steadily pushed Emily up against his own shoulder and slowly began to walk her up the hill. "See we're going to get there. Whether we find them or not, you need serious help."

"Mental or physical?" Emily sighed and tried hard to match his pace as the ground levelled out. Suddenly, the monument stood in front of them. John pulled her back from the large stone staircase and battered flowerbeds towards a set of steps. He stared down them wondered just how long their descent would take with Emily hobbling and barely able to stand. Movement in the low bushland caught his eye and he stepped back a little. Emily groaned in discomfort as pain coursed through her body. John glanced down and registered Emily's deteriorating condition. Without a word, he started to walk her down the opposite side, following a winding path which would take them around the outskirts of the park, avoiding whatever lurked in the shadows in wait for them.

As they moved, the sound of the wind blowing through the trees was mixed with the crunch of leaves and the twisting of roots. Limping on, Emily looked up to take in her surroundings. Unsure of what she was seeing, she inhaled deeply.

"What the fuck is that?" John spun to face whatever Emily had seen. Thick tentacles connected to the base of a tree, twisting viciously around its roots, and ending inside of the trunk. These tentacles protruded out of the tree, thin and needle-like they pierced not one, but several, bodies.

To their horror, the eyes of one of the cruelly captured humans flickered open, its mouth making a sickening tearing sound as it called out, "Heeere booooy. . .wheeere are you boooy?"

As if awakened, more and more voices echoed the call, each with its own script to follow.

"I wiiiiill push youuu Charlieeee, daddy's heeere."

"Nooo, no. What are yoooou doiiing to meee?"

The pair of them quickly turned and moved further down the line. Each voice left behind a disturbing ringing in their ears, their final words leaving a haunting imprint on them as they fled. Pushing through her pain and trying hard to block out the sounds of the tormented souls in the once peaceful park, Emily hobbled on. Eventually they reached the park exit and Emily pushed off John's shoulder and fell hard to ground.

"Hey what are. . ?"

"Just stop. . . please." Emily leaned awkwardly on her torn leg, "I can't do this!" She put her head in her hands and screamed hard.

"Woah, hold on, Emily," John leaned down and tried to comfort her but found her fist brushing against his face.

"No! I'm. . ." Emily dragged her hands down her face. She couldn't help but think about the fact that she had been sick;

she had given off all the hallmarks of an infected individual. What was she going to do if she was reunited with her children? They wouldn't want to be with their clearly sick mother.

John placed his hand on her shoulder, "Hey, come on." He put his other hand under her chin and lifted her head to reveal a mess of hair and tears, "You can do this. You have to. You've survived so much already. Clearly you have some determination left in you or you wouldn't be here with me." Emily sat and breathed in as deeply as she could, letting out all of her emotion in a breath. She sat there and shook her head.

"Come on. We should stop, I think from the looks of things, we can get five minutes." Emily nodded and dragged herself across the battered tarmac, slumping against the perimeter fence. All she wanted was the warm embrace of her family, for them all to be together again.

Chapter 9

Emily had gradually become more hunched over. She rested her forehead on her knees, deciding it would be best not to fall asleep next to a complete stranger, in a dark and utterly horrific park.

"Hey John, have you got any paper?"

John turned with a raised brow, "Excuse me?"

"Pen and paper, do you have any?"

John opened his backpack and rattled around between the supplies inside to produce the items she'd asked for, "Yeah, why?"

Emily reached out and took the paper, pulling it towards her, "Do you mind if I have it?"

"No, I guess not."

Emily painfully pushed her legs out and rested the pad against them. Flipping the generic cover open, putting the pen to the paper, and starting to write –

Children. I am so sorry. I didn't do enough to protect you. I didn't do enough to get us to your Dad.

She squeezed the pen as she felt herself welling up inside.

I hope I can get this diary to you and, when I do, you will know how much I love you. And Jack, I really hope you're still alive.

Emily continued. John tried not to peak too much but found

himself confused by her need to write. He held his tongue long enough for her to roll the cover back over and to have the pad pushed back under his nose.

"Thank you," Emily smiled under her mask and held out her hand, "Shall we go?" John nodded, tugging on her arm, causing her agony, as she staggered back to her feet. The pair walked steadily into what was the beginning of a new day. Smoke filled the foggy air, but the sun left an orange gleam across the horizon to light the way as they stumbled back on track down the town's long main road. No longer under the cover of darkness, they would need to be more careful this time to avoid any further interruptions.

As they slowly made their way up the hill, it was clear that most of the activity was in the town centre; the outer areas didn't seem, for the moment, as threatening. Emily imagined unseen dangers as she limped fearfully onwards. It was clear not many had made it to safety, or out of the area at all. The dead lay in nearby cars, their bodies displaying the wounds from a recent attack. Dark coloured liquid trailed from some of the vehicles, dripping onto the ground below. The bodies were drained of bodily fluids; it was as though it had been drawn out of them. Questions filled Emily's head, but nothing seemed to slow John down as he kept his eyes forward and his pace steady. She wondered what had happened to him during all this, had he lost someone, was he just playing the hero? None of that really mattered, she had to be selfish, she had her family to reunite.

Reaching the top of the hill, the sun caught the pair off guard. John raised his arm to cover his eyes as Emily kept her head down, unable to lift her arm higher than her waist. They stopped briefly and took in the view; a scene of genuine beauty was mixed with horror. The devastation they could see gave the moment a dark feeling, they could imagine the feeling of panic in the air as everyone moved frantically in an attempt to escape. Ultimately, their mission was to prove futile as they met their end.

Emily, having been in hiding at the school at the time, couldn't resist the urge to ask about when all the destruction had begun, "John, what happened when it all started?"

"It was chaos!"

"When it happened, me and my children hid in their school. We didn't move until well into the night."

"I was working at the Abbey. Suddenly, there were a few crashes nearby. No one thought anything of it until the text came. People bolted in every direction. The staff and a few of the visitors hid in the catacombs underneath. Besides that, I don't really know." John pulled Emily up and picked up the pace, "Then the monsters appeared and well. . . you know the rest." Emily winced. Sensing John's discomfort, she decided to cease her questioning.

It was eerily quiet as they continued to move between the rows of trees. Further down the road the destruction became increasingly evident; windows were smashed, glass littered the floor, homes had been ransacked, doorways were completely broken-down revealing horrors within. How could there be so few people remaining in the town? With all the cars left behind, surely somebody got out and, even if nobody did, where are all the bodies? Emily repeatedly pushed the same question from her mind; was Jack dead?

Crossing the road, they crunched through window glass and rubbish blowing freely in the wind. John slowed to a stop. Emily followed his gaze and saw a group of survivors moving in the distance. John's face turned pale as he pulled her along and twisted her awkwardly around, using a battered car for cover. They peered around the car and watched as a group of six moved steadily, in a formation between the cars, to create a line across the street. John spun round and hit the ground with his fist.

"Shit, we can't stay here. We have to get off the street now!"

"Why, who are they?"

"Not now, we have to go, follow me, stay low and don't make a sound." Emily nodded and they both moved in a low crouch across the floor, heading towards the street opposite which would act as a shortcut to the shelter. John moved quickly, scrambling up against the street wall and waving frantically at Emily to move faster. As she tried to obey, she stumbled on her injured foot and slipped on some glass, scratching her hand.

"Oh f. . ." she held her breath as she sprawled across the floor, landing with a clatter.

John spotted that the group had already began to move in on them. "Emily, move! Come on!" He scrambled back to her and pulled her up; they headed for the house nearby. The door to the house was still intact and closed with a reassuring click behind them. John stood as Emily painfully brushed the glass from her hand, shedding it on to the stained carpet.

"I'm sorry, I couldn't. . ."

"Stop, it's fine. Just go, move!" John turned the key in the lock as the group outside muttered quietly, trying to find an easy way in. The door was continuously beaten in an attempt to gain access. John and Emily moved at speed through the house finding themselves in the large kitchen, littered with utensils and debris discarded by the last lot of looters. John leaned heavily against the kitchen door in a desperate attempt to hold it closed.

"Emily, duck!" Emily did as she was told and dropped to the

floor, the action sending agonising pain coursing through her body. Looking up, she saw that one of the group had thrown a brick, breaking the large kitchen window, and was now making his way in. A rush of adrenaline gave her the strength to move. She grabbed a nearby pan, slamming the intruder in the side of the head. As he fell to the ground, she laid into him again. The intruder screamed; he was bleeding heavily from his nose. The door swung open allowing another of the group to enter but, in the confusion, John managed to land a well-placed fist on the man's face. He watched him drop to his knees. Pulling Emily along with him, John stumbled up the stairs just the front door gave way to the others in the group.

"Emily, in here, come on!" John pulled her into a nearby room and slammed the door shut.

Emily took a moment to take in her surroundings. It was a child's room, much like her son's. It was filled with toys and books, the floor littered with bedding and clothes. Blood and bile stained everything. John pulled her aside and placed a finger on his lip. Emily nodded. She moved over to a built-in wardrobe, pulling the doors open and stepping inside. Leaning her back against the wall, she took a moment's respite.

The sound of footsteps put her back on full alert. Doors along the house's corridor were brutally kicked in. Emily found it strange that none of the intruders had spoken, they simply moved in a formation, like a team. Was it all planned? The bedroom door swung viciously open, and bounced off the wall, as one of the intruders strode inside. Luckily, the door did enough to cover John as he stood behind it, waiting for his moment. The intruder walked cautiously inside, knowing John and Emily had to be in this final room. Anxiously, Emily clutched at the carpet beneath her. She twitched as the door closed and John darted at the intruder, smashing him against the bedroom window. John's fist hit his attacker in the face causing him to hold his head in agony.

"Emily, go downstairs!" She stumbled out of the room and back down the corridor. John followed close behind. "Back through the kitchen, through the door!" he instructed.

Moving over the mess they'd contributed to; Emily was greeted by an arm knocking her backwards. She stared directly at one of the intruders. Pinned to the floor she struggled, screaming beneath her mask, trying to find the energy to shift her attacker. Grabbing a pan, she struck him across the head allowing her just enough time to roll over and start crawling across the floor. Her attacker spun around and grabbed her leg, holding it in a painful grip as Emily desperately tried to wriggle free. She pulled along the cold, blood-soaked tiles, scrabbling for a knife. Kicking out with her free leg to distract him, she made one final lunge for the large knife and, wrapping her hand firmly around it, swung round and plunged it deep into her attacker's arm.

As Emily was promptly released, his scream rang out across the house. He held his arm in agony, blood spewing from the wound. John moved in to aim another punch, but everyone was stopped dead in their tracks as the roar of something extremely close by rose above the noise of the frantic fighting. The intruders took one look at each other, simply nodding and then making a break for the kitchen door. Bolting out of the house they bounded over the wall, the blood trail showing their escape route.

"We should go too," John pulled Emily up and they made for the same exit. The sound of glass crunching underfoot made them prick up their ears and they both forced themselves to move faster, away from whatever monster was approaching.

John bore Emily's weight as they moved, the morning sun rose as their destination came into sight. The old house stood bravely, but battered, before the entrance, the curtains blowing freely in the light, refreshing breeze. The field to the side lay barren and lifeless Emily recalled farm animals grazing there; Kyle would love to tell her that when the cows sat down it meant it would rain. A smile played on her lips as she realised just how close she might be to finding her children again, though it faltered slightly as she wondered just how they would react to seeing her, after all she was okay, wasn't she?

Through the archway, the Abbey appeared in the clearing, its large, red stones revealing its history. Scaffolding surrounded the building; love and attention had been spent on it in order to preserve it and ensure its survival. They stepped up to the perimeter fence and John rattled it gently, releasing a bolt on the gate and allowing Emily to step onto the well-kept grass. John continued to support Emily as they continued on through the grounds.

As they walked on, large archways greeted them, a vast and open green space overlay what had once been the rooms of the abbey. Stairways ended abruptly and thin metal gates restricted visitors from accessing dangerous areas. John guided Emily on through the grounds until they reached a thin metal fence. John pulled a section aside to allow them both just enough room to squeeze in.

"The shelter's in here. Come on, you really look like you need a rest."

Emily stood uneasily at the entrance as she stared at the opening of the large room; low lit lamps provided some light, but the space remained gloomy.

"Come on Emily, you. . ." John let go of the fence. As he began to move back to her, her eyes rolled, and she collapsed to the ground. He carefully moved her onto her side and wrapped his arms around her. Carrying Emily, John sidestepped through the fence and entered into the shadowy shelter. The dim lighting illuminated the way into the deepest part of the abbey, the catacombs.

Chapter 10

Kyle scrubbed furiously at the paper with his chunky green crayon, the lettering and frame of the plaque underneath made it tricky to really get it perfect. He stopped, let out a huge sigh of relief and brushed his hand across his brow.

"Oh, wow! That is so cool! Hey Amy look at this!" Kyle proudly held up his rubbing of the plaque. Amy lifted her head and gave him a thumbs-up. She was envious of his ability to switch off at a moment's notice; his natural curiosity made it easier for him to forget the situation they were in. In some ways it frustrated her, but, at the same time, she was glad of it. She often thought about what their mum would do - how would she keep them safe? How would she keep them from fighting for no good reason? Then reality would hit as she realised that their Mum wasn't there, it was just the two of them now. Amy had no plan; by a twist of circumstance, they had been rescued, but it didn't feel like the safety she wanted for them both.

The catacombs under the Abbey were dark, their appearance and atmosphere unwelcoming. Weak lighting lit up the main corridors that were used by the residents of the shelter. Various rooms used for storage and general seating or waiting lead off from it. Amy soon got the message that she should stick to these areas; the general feeling was that children shouldn't be wandering around aimlessly.

Kyle had made a companion of one of the members of staff who had shown him the truly exciting art of pencil-rubbing. He delighted in the knowledge that any imprint could be copied with a big chunky crayon. His enthusiasm hadn't waned, not yet anyway.

"Amy, look. Look I did more!" Kyle thrust large pieces of paper into her face.

"Wow, Kyle. These are cool."

"Yeah, I'm just going copy everything until this crayon is smushed from all the colouring!" Kyle laughed happily to himself. "Excuse me, do you have more paper?" Kyle turned to the woman who had sat with him, bouncing around with enjoyment.

"Of course, I think one of my friends got some when you guys arrived. Amy, do you mind getting some for your brother, might be nice to stretch your legs?" The woman stood and took big strides towards her, she was very tall and moved quickly, "I'll show you where to go." Amy nodded and got to her feet to follow the woman out of the room. "Head to the end of here, the lights will stop so you will know not to keep going, the paper is in a little storage room on your left."

Amy put on the slightly large hoodie she had been given when she had arrived; her original clothes were damp and dirty, she was glad to at least change some part of them. The fact she hadn't washed or changed properly in days filled her with disgust.

She slowly shuffled down the corridor, her hands tucked deep into the hoodie's large pockets, clasping them together in an attempt to keep herself calm. The place was creepy, the way the lights flickered randomly, corridors led off into total blackness and something about staring into the dark had her imagination in overdrive. As she reached the end of the corridor, she brushed against the wall and turned into the storage room. Inside was a hastily assembled supply room full of various sized cardboard boxes stuffed with all kinds of items. Nothing was organised so, with a big sigh, Amy moved into the room and started to search for what she wanted.

Releasing her hands from the comfort of the pockets, she tore open the first box to reveal food ration packets and chocolate bars obviously raided from a vending machine. She took a quick look over her shoulder and pulled one from the box, slowly opening it as quietly as she could and taking a bite. The chocolate didn't last long, but the feeling of some food and the sugar-rush it gave her was welcome. She quickly packed the box back up and moved along the room to see what else she could find. Between the masks, filters and various historical items, nothing really stood out for her until a quiet hum, which echoed briefly on and off, stopped her in her tracks. Amy stood still, trying to figure out what the noise was. Again, it would hum, stop, and carry on. Intrigued, she moved to the doorway and glanced from side to side. Again, the repeated rhythm echoed fleetingly. Her heart sank as she realised the noise came from somewhere in the darkness beyond. She considered for a moment if it was worth pursuing it and wondered what her mum would do. Knowing the answer, she took a bold step in to the blackness.

As she walked slowly, she peered over her shoulder for, what felt like, a hundred times. The light from the main corridor just about carried her around the corner where she suddenly found herself in a room. Stepping further inside, she tripped over an object that lay on the floor. Crawling on her hands and knees, she trembled with fear. The hum began once again; this time she knew she had found the source of where the noise was coming from. The room lit up momentarily and Amy's face did too, with excitement. She jumped over what turned out to be a backpack laid on the floor, wrestling quickly with it and producing a smartphone.

"Yes! Thank you, thank you!" she rejoiced as she held the phone. Pushing on its screen, she was met with a number pad. Checking over her shoulder again, she looked back at the phone and quickly tapped in a six-number combination, the one she hoped was correct. The phone buzzed. As she stared at it, some extra icons showing a torch, camera and phone were visible. She smiled beneath her mask and tapped the phone icon. This could be her chance to find her Dad and to get some real help, to feel safe. Then it dawned on her - she didn't actually know his number. Her hand dropped as she let out a sigh of disappointment. She wondered if he was even alive anyway. As the phone slipped, the room lit up allowing its contents to be seen. Amy looked up and around in amazement, there must have been ten or twenty backpacks piled up randomly.

She tapped the torch icon and lit up the room properly to reveal its entire contents. As she spun around, something wasn't quite right. Dotted around the room, on the backpacks and on the floor and walls were red stains, dark even in the torchlight. Amy let go of the phone which landed camera-side down, plunging the room into darkness again. She fumbled her way towards the exit. On leaving, she bumped into the woman who'd been with her brother earlier.

"Hey, I said the room before the lights go out," she stood peering over Amy's shoulder, "You don't want to go back there, it's really dark. I don't think they finished making the whole place safe. Stick to the lights, okay?" Amy nodded her head quickly.

She returned to Kyle who turned towards her, disappointment showing on his face.

"Hey, where's the paper?" he asked.

"Sorry, I err couldn't find any."

"Oh well, where's Mum's backpack?"

Amy stopped and thought for a second

"Mum had some paper, didn't she?" Kyle persisted.

"She did, but that was her. . ."

"Hey Kyle, it's here." The children turned to look at the woman standing again in the doorway, this time holding the backpack Amy had taken from their Mum when they'd run from her.

"Oh yeah! Paper!" Kyle celebrated.

Amy frowned and moved quickly to take the backpack from the woman. "This was my Mum's. I'll look after it." She dropped to her knees and quickly searched around inside. Nothing was missing. Amy turned and smiled, "Thanks, I'll give Kyle some paper."

"Great. Well, I'll be around. Don't wander off, okay?" The children smiled and nodded as she left the room. Amy turned to the backpack and pulled her Mum's diary from it.

"Hey, come on. Please can I have some paper now?" demanded Kyle. Amy huffed and flicked to the back of the notebook, tearing a handful of pages out and pushing them towards her brother, who cheered and moved back into the room to continue his drawing.

With Kyle content, Amy turned the notebook back to the front cover and decided to peer inside to read what her Mum had written, to maybe understand what she was going through trying to protect them. She slowly turned to the first page and steadily began to read:

Dear diary. This sucks.

Amy let out a little laugh, the first line already reminded her of her Mum's humour. She read on and took a moment to appreciate how hard it must have been for her Mum, for her to have put them first, to protect them from something so dangerous, whilst, all the time, knowing she might never see her husband again. Amy wasn't one for love and emotion, but it really hit her hard. A tear ran down her cheek, she quickly wiped it away with the long sleeve of her oversized hoodie. As she rubbed her eyes, Kyle appeared in front of her with a puzzled look.

"Are you okay?" Kyle enquired.

"Hmm, I am yeah, just missing Mum. That's all," his sister replied.

"Do you think she's okay?"

"I-I don't know. I hope so. Do you want to come and write something for mum?" Kyle's eyes widened and he nodded quickly. As he slipped under her arm, Amy felt, for just a moment, that little bit safer.

"Okay Kyle, go into the backpack and grab me a pen, I bet mum stole one from the library." Kyle moved quickly, grabbing his prize and running back to slip under Amy's arm again.

"Okay, so what to write. . . hmm I know. *Dear Mum, wherever you may be, we are safe because of you. We ran as fast as we could and found help. We miss you.*" Amy put the pen down and turned to Kyle, "What do you think?"

"Yeah, that's great!"

"Do you mind if I just write something by myself?" Kyle nodded and walked away, grabbing his battered crayons once more and going back to his art.

Amy put pen to paper and began to write again:

I know you did not have a choice to leave us. We love you the all the same, I promise.

Amy continued to write a little more before the sound of footsteps and shouting echoing from the halls came back to them. Kyle and Amy headed to the doorway and peered down the long corridor. At the entrance were lots of bodies and people moving around in a panicked state. As they watched, a man steadily walked down the crumbling staircase, he was carrying a woman in his arms. Another man took the woman from him and moved her into one of the rooms.

"Amy, who do you think that is? Could it be mum?" Amy stood in silence; a thousand thoughts ran through her head. If it was their mother, they could all be in danger.

Chapter 11

Emily groaned as she slowly came back to reality. As she attempted to open her eyes, she found herself continuously blinking as she tried to work out where she actually was. After a moment of panic, she placed her arm behind herself and pushed forwards; a sharp pain travelled up her back, so she lay back down to rest. The pain moved through her back and up to her skull, it was such an intense headache she couldn't help but put her hands to her head. She tried to smooth her hair, finding it matted together with a mixture of mud and blood. As she untangled her fingers, a man entered the room.

"Hey, how was the nap?" It was John, "I don't want to be rude but you're looking awful."

"Wow, good morning to you too."

"You're welcome. I mean, I'm impressed you have some fight in you. How are you holding up?"

"I'm not tired anymore," she laughed awkwardly as she slowly examined herself from the makeshift bed she had ended up on, "I seem to be neatly bandaged up? When did that. . .?"

"One of the staff is first aid trained, she bandaged you up, nothing more we could do, just hoped you would wake up."

"Well, thank you for the help and for getting me here, it means a lot. Nice to stop again, actually."

Emily twisted uncomfortably as she stared up at the ceiling, trying to remember the last time she had felt safe and appreciating the few minutes of peace.

"So, remind me, where the hell are we?"

"We are under the Abbey, in the old catacombs that stood beneath it this entire time. It was going to be quite the reveal when we had finally opened it all up."

"Suppose it's pretty isolated. Nobody would know to come here to rob you, I guess."

John laughed as he leant against the wall, "That's true, we've done well so far."

"How long exactly has it been since this all started?" Emily wriggled in discomfort as she attempted again to lay in a comfortable position.

"Well, it's early now," John rolled up his sleeve and checked the digital watch on his wrist, it looked a lot like a fitness tracker, "It's one in the morning to be precise so... about 5 days. This is day five."

"Day five and we are still living like this? Where is the army, the-?" as she began her verbally assault another man appeared and tapped John on the shoulder.

"Excuse me, I see our guest is alive and well so to speak."

"Yes, this is Emily. Emily, this is David, he is the curator of the Abbey."

Emily eyed the man, towering in the doorway, from a distance. In the dim lighting of the corridor, the man looked to be part of the shadows, his light white hair shining strangely in the darkness.

"It's nice to meet you and to know you're safe. John told me about the encounter that brought you and him together. You're lucky we had him out there with all those lunatics and monsters running wild. I shudder to think what the outcome might have been otherwise."

"Yeah I-"

"He also told me you were separated from your children."

Emily strained to sit upright, "You know them? Are they here? Are they safe?"

The old man laughed and stepped inside allowing his shadow to disappear, "Our other scavenger came across two children who talked about being separated from their mother and, well, I guess this is the hero herself?"

Emily slumped back, "Where are they?"

"The children in question are asleep and I think it would be good for them to rest just a little longer. Why don't you come with me and I'll give you a tour while you're awake? This place is fantastic and full of history, enough to keep your head busy anyway. Come, come." David stepped back and held out his arm pointing to the door, smiling beneath his mask.

Emily didn't trust this man. She didn't even trust John; he'd spent the whole time sitting there saying nothing at all. Something felt wrong. She twisted her body off the bed and put her feet on the ground. Her shoes were scuffed, battered and blood-soaked.

The curator led the way as Emily followed him down the corridor until they came to the point where the lighting abruptly ended. David reached around the corner and picked up a large lamp tucked away into a hole in the wall. Pushing the switch with a loud click, the darkness vanished as the lamp completely lit the way, revealing how much further the corridor went and the number of rooms which sat side by side.

"So, Emily, if it helps, this place is vast. We have yet to truly unearth all of its secrets, some are really quite frightening but intriguing at the same time."

Emily found herself tensing as the old curator move on. The walls had been crudely carved, but it was impossible to tell what instrument had made the strange markings on them. The further they walked, the more unusual the carvings became. The tiling leading onwards changed in colour and the atmosphere felt airless.

"The monks of this place kept to themselves at first before they started trading with the nearby villagers. They were a fair tradesman, dealing in all kinds of items that hadn't seen in the area before. Somewhere along the way, this large catacomb was built under the Abbey and acted as a secret trading post, allowing the monks to move freely, away from prying eyes, to various key points in what we now call Cumbria."

The curator slowed to a stop and placed the lamp down as they reached a large, mosaic-covered door. The markings on the door gave a dark vibe; the markings of fighting and violence were clear.

"The monks had a secret under here and we found it, let me show you." He twisted the centre of the mosaic and the lock released allowing him to pull the doors apart. Besides the dust being whipped up by the sudden inrush of air, an uneasy feeling seemed to emanate from the room.

"Come, come. Look, it's quite the marvel" David ushered Emily inside. Retrieving his lamp, he held it up to reveal the incredible architecture of the room. The walls were covered in a large mosaic similar to that on the entrance door, the depiction was violent in nature. Emily felt increasingly sick as she began to realise the danger she was in.

"What is this room?" she asked.

"This is the room that the monks kept hidden from the

local people, the room that even kings feared, hence why they destroyed the Abbey above. They had uncovered something truly amazing, something that could change opinions and instill dread in others, allowing them control over the outside world."

"But, I mean, what is it? And weren't monks supposed to be holy?"

"Not these monks. They had made a deal with something."

"And what was that something?" She brushed her hands along the benching which sat perfectly preserved beside her.

"Take a look."

Emily turned. David had lifted the lamp up to a large statue. It was carved from wood and stood towering over the room, its presence commanding. It appeared to be wearing a long cloak, its horned antlers piercing through the top of its head.

"Jesus, what is that?"

"It, Emily, has been called many things, but I believe it to be a woodland demon of some sort. Its shrine was built here so that those who later uncovered it could take control, like the monks had done before them. Now we have command of the site; we have an incredible power before us, we just have to harness it."

Emily moved slowly backwards, she felt completely helpless as she listened to the curator's mad rant. As she turned to test her escape route, a man entered the room and hovered in the doorway, not blocking it but it was enough to show her that he didn't intend to let her leave without an escort.

"Okay, so how do you intend to harness this power? I don't really get what you're telling me."

"I'm not a hundred percent sure but I think you're the key, Emily."

"Excuse me?" she held her hands up, "Woah, hang on. What do you mean?"

"Let's find out."

David nodded to the man at the door, who briefly stepped out and ushered more people into the room. Emily dropped to her knees in a mixture of joy, relief and disbelief as her children entered.

"Kids! What are-?" Emily struggled for words as a hundred questions ran through her head.

"Mum! Mum!" Kyle screamed as he ran towards her, hugging her as hard as he could. They both shed a tear or two, "Oh Mum, I knew you were okay."

"I am, I'm okay, I promise. I'm so sorry I-," she squeezed her son tightly and could barely get her words out as she lifted her head to find her daughter standing nearby, unsure of what to do, "Amy? Amy, it's okay. Look, I'm fine, I promise, look!"

Amy stepped forward slowly, her arms wrapped around her own body.

"Mum?"

"It's okay, I promise. Come here, I missed you!" Emily opened her arms and Amy fell into her embrace.

Their family reunion was broken up by the slow clapping that echoed around the room. Emily lifted her head and found David leaning down towards them.

"This is why you're the key. You, the one who got infected by the curse and survived. You are the one sent for us. For me!"

David waved a finger down and Emily found herself against the floor as everything turned black once again.

Chapter 12

Emily came to, feeling a sharp pain in the head, she winced and wriggled her jaw. She tried to move but quickly became panic-stricken as she realised that her hands were tied. She again found herself on her knees, this time not embraced by her children but hearing their whimpers in the background, as she remembered where she was. Slowly lifting her head, she found herself looking directly at the creepy statue she had been introduced to earlier.

Flicking her head from side to side she called out, "Kids? Amy! Kyle!"

"Mum we're here!" Emily spun her head to her left and found her crying children being clutched by two men; they wore similar cloaks to the disturbing statue, their faces completely masked.

"David!"

"Emily, you're awake. Perfect, you can bear witness to what will save us!"

"You bastard, let me go right now!"

"Oh Emily, I couldn't do that. You are the one who will end this nightmare. We will bargain for our survival by using your blood."

"Like hell you will! You're a mad man! Let me go right now

before I break your neck!"

"Never. I'm in charge here. And I shall remain so."

Emily stumbled to her feet and made a move towards the curator, but a swift kick to her leg had her falling hard to the floor. The children screamed as their mother hit the ground; Amy tried in vain to get free from her captor.

"Mum, get up please!"

"Yes Emily, get up, we have much to do. Stop playing the fool." David stepped up to a stone tablet behind the statue, a lighter burning bright in his hand, "We will begin preparations for its arrival. Now, stop fighting or I will do what I must." David nodded to the figures holding her children, beneath their cloaks the held blades.

"No, please wait. Not them, you have me. Let them go free!"

"Not until the ritual is complete! Now, do as you're told, and I will release your hands. Then we can begin."

Emily closed her eyes, inhaling through her nose and breathing out through her mouth. Opening her eyes again, she nodded her head.

"Mum, wait, no!"

"It's okay kids. Please," she held out her hands and David smiled. She noticed he wasn't wearing a mask this time. He meant business, hellbent on carrying out his sick ritual. David revealed his own blade and steadily cut the rope that he had used to bind her hands. Free, she fought the urge to clench her fist and place it right into the curator's chest, but she knew that wouldn't get her or her children anywhere.

"Now Emily, take the lighter from the table and light the torch in front of you. You will light the unholy bindings before you and around the room."

Emily slowly lit the torches and began to take stock of the

room in all its incredibly ugly glory. Where she stood, lines and curves in a circular pattern carved into the stone lead to the statue in the room. The walls were covered in murals depicting a violent clash and she had to angle her head downwards to avoid having to look at the mosaic gorefest that layered the walls.

Reaching the final torch, she held the lighter to it and then clicked the lid shut, swiftly pushing it into her pocket. As she stood there, she noticed the room was filling with smoke. Nobody seemed concerned by this, but the lack of ventilation was surely going to become a problem. The smell of something scented swiftly filled her nose and she suddenly felt faint.

"Return to us, Emily, we are not done."

She stepped back onto the stone carving. A sick feeling rose within her as she realised what was coming next. David continued to preach to his people. Emily began to sway, she felt almost weak as she moved gently from side to side.

Suddenly, she found herself staring at a blade and she snapped, her breathing becoming laboured. She flailed her arms, shoving David back into the statue and knocking the torch to the ground. As it landed, an even heavier cloud of smoke was created. Emily stood stunned as she watched David pull himself back to his feet.

"You bit-,"

His face changed and he dropped to his knees, "Oh great one, it is you!"

Emily spun around to stare at the shadow that rose up the wall and couldn't help but scream. As if she had given a command, everyone in the room followed her lead and also began screaming, waving their hands violently, blades scraping as they lunged at each other. In an instant the room was in total chaos.

Emily shook her head, her eyes closed, and she counted herself back in, "One. Two. Three. Four. Five."

She turned to find her children curled into a ball in the corner of the room.

"Come on, we have to go it's going to be okay. Just move, don't look!"

Emily pulled the children off the floor and pushed them towards the door, following as closely as she could. Stumbling out into the corridor, she grabbed her confused children.

"Okay, come on we-," as she attempted to take control of the situation, a shadow caught her eye. The longer she stared, the more it moved, and, with every move, a shiver ran up her spine. The shadow stepped slowly out of the wall and stood tall in front of the exit, letting out a scream.

"Run!" Emily turned, grabbing Kyle, and heading out into the dark corridor. After a few paces she turned to find Amy wasn't there, "Amy? Amy! Wait!"

Amy had decided to sprint at the shadow, diving into one of the rooms she had found herself in earlier and lying on the floor. Emily tried to go back for her daughter, but the shadow moved slowly towards her. She grabbed Kyle's arm and ran deeper into the dark.

Figuring it was safe to do so, Amy lifted her head. Slowly, she tried to make out her surroundings in the dark, fumbling with the bags that littered the room. As she crawled across the floor, she grabbed at what she thought was a smartphone and quickly felt around for the pocket zip. Eventually she was successful, she unzipped the pocket and pulled the smartphone from it, the light from the screen brightening the room enough for her to locate the torch. With a light in hand, she decided to look for her Mum's backpack. They were going to get out, she just had to find this bag, it was important.

Amy pulled and kicked at the bags in the room as she desperately tried to find their backpack. One bag came open, a notebook poked out from the top, the pen skating across the floor.

"Yes! Come here!" Amy scrabbled on the floor, stuffed the notebook back into the bag and grabbed the pen. As she closed the zip around the backpack and pulled it on, a shadow stood motionless in the doorway. Amy shook as she held the torch towards it. Suddenly, monster shrieked and jumped at her, Amy let out a scream and closed her eyes. When she opened her eyes a few seconds later, it was gone, she was safe. Without a second thought, she made a move for the door and, with the torch in hand, made a break for the dark corridor.

"Hold on, Mum. I'm coming!"

Emily and Kyle had slowed as the darkness began to engulf them and found themselves running their hands along the rough stone walls. Emily leaned into her son to get him to walk on. She was having a struggle to breathe.

"Mum, where are we?"

"I don't know but we have to keep going." Emily pushed her hand onto Kyle's shoulder and tried to guide him onwards, his slow and steady sobbing rang through the corridor like a bell. "Kyle, I know you're scared but I need you to try to stop, please."

"But Mum, I'm scared." Kyle spluttered and stopped, "Mum, where's Amy?"

"I don't know but we need to be quiet."

"No, I want Amy, I want Dad!"

"Kyle," Emily lowered herself down to Kyle's height and held him in a tight embrace, his sobbing becoming a cry as he let it all out, "I'm sorry, I am."

Emily stopped for a moment and tried to comfort her son but slowly she too began to well up. She found a steady trail of tears running down her face and into her son's damp and clammy hair, Emily pushed herself deeper into his shoulder and Kyle squeezed her in return. In the distance, noises clattered along the corridor and echoed in their ears, Emily tensed and opened her eyes. Nothing. Emily flicked her head side to side frantically trying to figure out what the noises were and where they were coming from. Was it footsteps? Noises back down the corridor from the chaos? Emily started to panic as the sounds continued to echo around the corridors, confusing her sense of direction. Suddenly they stopped.

"Mum–?"

"Shh," Emily put her hand over Kyle's mouth and the pair sat there motionless in the darkness. The quiet was almost as alarming as the noise had been. Emily strained her ears to pick up any sound, her hand tensing into a fist as the noise started again and she prepared to fight for their lives. Again, it stopped. When it began once more, Emily let go of her son and placed her hand over her ear, slowly rotating her head, trying to pinpoint where the noise was coming from. As she slowly turned, her body froze, a cold shiver running down her back as the noise appeared to be directly next to her ear. It clicked repeatedly and let out a cracking noise like something had broken; Emily inhaled sharply, and she placed her free hand over her own mouth trying desperately not to scream. Whatever was hunting them was directly beside her, dread filled her as she heard the sound of the being exhaling. It was close, she could sense what had to be a lengthy arm arch its way across their heads and reach out behind Kyle. Emily screamed, flailing as she spun round.

"Go away!" Emily screamed as she swung her arms, falling

and landing on Kyle's foot. The hunter in the dark let out a scream as a light lit up the corridor and blinded them both.

"Mum? Mum! Kyle!"

Emily held her arm up to block out the light and leaned in.

"Amy? Amy, is that you?"

The light lowered enough to allow Emily to look up without shielding her eyes and, to her relief, her daughter stood in front of her, "Oh my god, Amy!" Emily jumped up and grabbed her daughter.

"Amy!" Kyle crawled over to his big sister, embracing her and squeezing her hard, "I knew you would find us."

"Amy, where did you get that light?"

"I found a phone earlier, before they brought you in. There were loads of bags in this room. They have to have brought others here."

"Well, whatever they're doing, I don't give a. . . let's get out of here. Which way do we go?" Emily stood as Amy turned and pointed back down the corridor, the way they had come through.

"We should go back, it's gone quiet. We could sneak through; we know the way."

Emily smiled as her daughter appeared so grown up, "Alright, I'll lead. Okay?"

Emily held out her hand and Amy placed the phone into it. Turning she started to wander back down the corridor with her children. Amy stood close to her brother and squeezing his hand tightly as she held on to the back of her mother's shirt. They walked steadily through the corridors, the torch on the phone cutting through the thick darkness.

Slowly the way became illuminated again and they stepped back into the aftermath of the earlier chaos. They all took a deep breath as they surveyed the blood-splattered floor and walls, drag marks painting the scene. Whatever had happened appeared to be over.

"Kids, don't look down, eyes to the door." Emily moved a little more hastily, the sound of her footsteps echoing in the corridor pushing her on.

"Mum, what happened? That didn't look like the monsters outside. I mean I saw a shadow literally walk off a wall."

"I don't know, Amy. I don't know what to say but we should concentrate on getting the hell out of here. Come on, there's the door. Go, get out!" Emily pushed Amy and Kyle onwards, watching as the pair sprinted for the derelict steps they had used to get into the catacombs. Emily turned to check for anyone trying to sneak up on them. The clicking noise pattered off the walls again. Emily hurried to the exit and ran to the stairs. Climbing them, she moved towards her children, who stood in the open green becoming drenched in the immense rainstorm that had gathered overhead whilst they were trapped down in the catacombs.

Emily slowed to a walk and looked to the sky, rubbing her hands over her face and across her hair, the feeling of rain against her body was welcome but her relief would be cut short.

"Mum!"

Emily found herself looking into the faces of her panic-stricken children who stumbled backwards. Turning, she slipped onto the floor and found herself wrestling for safety on the boggy ground. The curator had managed to escape and was twisting her body into the grass, his hands pushing her face into the waterlogged mud.

"Look what you have done! You angered them, now they are all dead! How many have died by your hand?"

As he continued to push her into the water, Emily twisted frantically trying to get away. The old curator might have looked feeble, but he had incredible strength. His robe clung to his body as the storm soaked him to the skin.

Seizing a chance to escape, Emily pushed herself up, slipping awkwardly. In shock, she saw that someone was standing over her attacker, hitting him over and over with a cricket bat. Her saviour beat him until he no longer had the energy to swing the bat, throwing it away and standing over the old man's body. Emily breathed hard as she stared at her rescuer, his raincoat soaked and covered in mud. As she wondered what might happen next, her children came to her side and held onto her tightly.

"Mum!" they both shouted, firmly squeezing Emily who slipped back on the mud as the man turned slowly and walked towards them.

"Look, get away, I don't want any trouble!"

"Hey, hey. Wait!" The man pulled down his hood to reveal his face, his black hair soaked from the wild storm, "It's me, it's Alan! Remember me?"

"Alan? What the-What are you doing here?"

"I was hiding out in some house along Abbey Road when I saw two kids with some guy. I didn't think anything of it till I recognised little Kyle and Amy in tow."

"Why didn't you help them?"

"I-I didn't know what to do."

"You mean to tell me you saw these two with some stranger and you didn't think to confront him or at least try to talk to them?"

"H-Hey, I'm sorry but everyone's gone fucking crazy."

"They could have died! What would Hayley say?"

Alan glanced to the side and twisted on the spot, "Hayley's dead Emily, so I don't know."

"Christ, I'm sorry I-"

"It's. . . Come on there's a house at the end of the road. Let's get out of the rain."

Alan held out his hand and pulled Emily up. He led them towards the broken fence they had used on their way in and back up the small road out. The rain had filled the drain outside of the old-fashioned house at the entrance. The four of them strode through the water without a second thought; Emily was thankfully to clean the blood from her shoes.

As they reached the house, Alan pushed his hand through the broken glass in the door, unbolted the lock on the back and twisted the handle. Taking a step inside, he ushered the others in, closing the door behind him. Emily stumbled into what could have been the living room, collapsing onto an old-fashioned sofa. She let her head lean back on its soft cushion and let out a sigh. At last, a bit of comfort. Her children followed her in and squeezed one under each arm. Enjoy the moment she thought, just enjoy the moment.

Chapter 13

Emily put her head in her hands, using the rain to clean her face.

Alan stood by the fireplace and shook his head, "Jesus what a bunch of psychos!"

"I know, right?"

"Do you think it was real?"

"Honestly, I have no idea and I don't really want to know." Emily looked over to her children who sat at an old dining table, "I'm just glad I got them back. I just need to find Jack now."

"Where is Jack anyway?"

"I don't really know. I was taking these two to school when it happened. I left him at home. It was his day off and he'd agreed to finish making the beds and things in the shelter."

"You think he got in there then?"

"I can only hope. I haven't been able to get in touch with him so... I just pray we don't find him dead somewhere," Emily squirmed and leaned her head down, "I'd rather not know, easier for them to think he's out there, somewhere."

"So, what's the plan now?"

"No idea."

"Hey, Mum, look I managed to save this." Amy had placed the backpack onto the table and pulled out the notebook from it, "I thought this might help."

Emily smiled and waved her hand, "Bring it here."

Amy pushed the chair across the floor and came to sit beside her Mum, putting the notebook into her hands, "We know you love us by the way." Emily bit her lip and planted a kiss on Amy's head then watched as her daughter went back to her chair at the dining table.

"What's that?"

"It's just something someone gave me. In the library, an old lady gave me a notebook and told me to write down my thoughts and feelings. Like a diary. It's helped me put things into perspective, I guess. Strange I know."

"Hey, we all have coping strategies. Mine's alcohol," Alan laughed and wandered to a single armchair to the side of the old sofa, "But I think we need to think of what to do next."

Emily pulled the pen from the side of the notebook and started to write, "I'm all ears should you have any ideas."

"Pfft, not really. Pretty useless, I let Hayley die."

Emily paused for a moment and glanced up to Alan who was holding back his own emotions, "Hey, I'm sure you did what you could."

"I hid. I hid like an effing coward." Alan hit the wall and glanced towards the startled children. He held up his hand and turned back to Emily, "I hid and. . . I heard it all. I can't do this."

Emily didn't know what to say; she knew how their ordeal had changed her. Her nature had become the complete opposite of what it used to be; it was not a change for the better. Above all, her instinct was to protect her children.

Alan shook his head and stared at the floor as Emily slowly put pen to paper again. In the quiet, few minutes she had, she found herself writing away in her little notebook before the sound of a truck filled the house.

"Woah, was that a truck?" Emily closed the notebook, got up and glanced through the small window in the front door. To her surprise, floodlights lit up the area not far from them and below them stood personnel wearing camouflage.

"What? When were you going to tell me that the army were here?"

"There's no way in hell I'm going over there, Emily. Do you know what they're doing?"

"Don't tell me you're being a damn conspiracy nut?"

"Emily, they've taken survivors, not to protect them, they've cuffed them and taken them... somewhere."

Emily looked back to the army camp outside and thought about everything they had endured so far. Was choosing to confront the military safe, or an absolutely dreadful idea?

"Well, if you won't go out there, then I will."

"Woah, there's not a chance I'm letting you go!"

"Try me! Seriously, I'm tired and I can't do this anymore. I can't live in fear of everyone in this town. Surely, they'll know we are not one of those things?"

"Are you not listening? They've forcibly taken people, Emily. This is not a trip back to find Jack, this is a god damn death wish!"

"Listen, if you want to sob in here, down a bottle of some poor old couple's alcohol stash, fine, go ahead, but I'm going out there and I'm going to get some help." Emily waved at her children, "Kids, pack the bag, we're going to get help." Emily turned to find Alan standing between her and the door.

"Please, I'm begging you, don't do this. I'll get you back into town, we can find Jack ourselves but please don't do this!"

"Alan, I'm going out that door and taking that chance." Emily stepped slowly towards him, "If they take us then, whatever the outcome, I could be one step closer to Jack. One step closer to us all being together. We've just endured nearly being killed by some cult under an Abbey, I think I'm ready to take a stab in the dark."

Alan shook his head, turned, twisted the handle, and opened the door to the storm. He walked past her without a second glance.

"I hope you're right then."

Emily watched as he ruffled the children's hair and took one last look at her, his eyes pleading with her not to go. Emily wrapped her arms around her children, took a deep breath and stepped out into the wild.

The three of them moved steadily toward the military checkpoint. Doubts filled her head, but she had made her decision and she was determined to stick to it. They followed the pavement, which was littered with brown and yellow leaves. They reached the top of the hill where the path met with the main road out of the town, in front of them stood the checkpoint. Emily stood for a moment and wondered how she hadn't noticed it on the way to the Abbey, but then she remembered she had detoured off the path early. Was it a coincidence? Was she really lured? No matter, she had survived, and she was going to be strong for the sake of her children.

"Come on you two. Stay close behind me and do not panic. These people are armed. Do you understand?"

The children nodded, and she turned back to the road and took the first step out. The closer she got to the checkpoint, the more fearful she became.

"Don't move!" In an instant the three of them were being

blinded by a searchlight. They all held up their hands to their faces, trying to shield their eyes, "Don't move or we will fire on you. Stay still!"

"Please, we need help!" Emily held her hands in the air and slowly stepped forward, "Please, I have children with me." As she took a step, a shot rang out, the sound clear even through the raging storm, the bullet ricocheting off the floor. Emily jolted back and waved her arms.

"Wait, don't shoot!" she held her arms to her sides and tried to keep her children from moving. Kyle was already cracking and ready to cry.

"Kids just hold on. It'll be okay I promise!" she shouted above the noise of the storm.

To the front a large group of soldiers were moving quickly towards her. They all wore large, dark green-coloured coats, their faces covered in huge gas masks. The soldiers moved around the three of them, each one holding an assault rifle.

"Please just stop, we're not infected. Look!" She stepped up to the lead soldier holding her arms out.

"Stop! Lie on your front. Now!" the soldier pointed his rifle to the floor to re-iterate his command.

"Please..."

"All of you, get down now! Restrain them." The lead soldier waved his hand and a handful of the others lowered their rifles, allowing them to sway from their chests, as they produced plastic restraints.

"Wait no, please!" Emily fell to the ground as she was hit hard in her back by a rifle. She landed face first, blood mixing with the rain, her arms drawn violently behind her as the restraints were pulled tight.

"What are you doing? Get off me! Get off my kids, you little fu-" Emily stopped abruptly as she received another blow to her head, knocking her out.

"Mum!" Amy screamed as her hands were tightly bound behind her whilst she watched the soldier hit her mother, "What are you doing?"

"Corporal, get us a transport." The lead soldier stood over the family as he issued his commands, "Radio ahead to the outpost that we have three civilians. Possible bios."

"Copy." The soldier moved from Amy and stepped back, pulling the radio on his chest.

"What did you do to my Mum, you idiots?"

"Shut up, kid. Get up now!" A soldier pulled her up by her restraints, her wrists burned, and she screamed in agony.

"What are you doing? Kyle! Kyle!" She squirmed in the soldier's arms as he held her to keep her from moving. She watched the soldiers pull Kyle to a stand. Her mother was laid at the feet of the squad leader who was waving to a vehicle which was heading towards them.

The vehicle was a huge military truck which was used to transport the soldiers. Amy had watched as they drove past earlier in the week, on the day it had all kicked off. She recalled the glares the soldiers gave her, even then.

Amy continued to wriggle in the soldier's arms.

"For fuck's sake kid, stop!" The soldier put his knee to the back of her leg, and she dropped suddenly, her arms lifted high behind her. She let out a scream as she found herself on her knees. Her tears mixed in with the rain streaming down her face.

As the transport pulled up in front of them, she found herself being commanded to get back on her feet. She scrabbled into the back of the vehicle, her brother slipped in beside her and they quickly sat down. The rain drummed against the material that covered the rear. They watched as their mother was hauled violently in with them and placed against the metal frame.

The soldiers talked together briefly, patting each other's shoulders. A group of five jumped into the back with the family and took a seat. The menacing look of the soldiers in their protective gear didn't stop Amy from glaring at them. One soldier hammered on the metal between the front and rear with his fist and with that the vehicle began to move. Amy stared at the floor, wondering if this was how it was going to end.

Chapter 14

Emily twitched as she awoke with a fright. She tried to put her hand to her face, panicking as she found herself bound and staring up at a fabric roof. Another bump brought her back to reality and she breathed a sigh of relief as she glanced around and saw her children.

"Oh, thank God. Kids, are you okay?" Amy and Kyle nodded, tears running down their faces.

"Hey, shut up!"

Emily shuffled painfully back along the soaked metallic floor.

"Kids, did they hurt you?"

"Oi, I said shut it!" Emily turned and found the military squad all beginning to shuffle in their seats, "Do I need to hit you again?"

"I dare you–"

"Oi, pair of you, shut it, alright?"

"How about you cut these restraints and do it again?" Emily twisted herself almost to a crouching position before stopping as the soldiers grabbed their rifles, the nearest already pointing his pistol towards her.

Emily slumped back down and tried to breathe in through her nose. The blood from her wounds flowed freely and was dripping steadily into her lap. She sat and wondered just what she had got herself into. As she pondered her predicament, the truck braked sharply, throwing her forward. She hit her head, the resulting bruise leaving her with a sharp pain in her head.

"Come on. . ."

"Alright you three, up and out. Don't do anything stupid or you will be shot. I will not tell you again."

The soldiers climbed out first, holding the fabric flap open and ushering them out. As they slowly stepped out, they were greeted by more searchlights and even more soldiers. Emily found a rifle pushed into her arm.

"Move!"

Emily slowly limped down the street, her children slightly ahead of her. She glanced up and took in her surroundings. The once busy street was now desolate and littered in debris, a handful of bullet casings shone in the sunlight. Looking ahead she followed the lines of the buildings and reached the top; they were at the town hall. Emily wondered why they were using this as an outpost. What the hell were they doing in restraints? Surely, the army were here to rescue them? Questions filled her head as she stepped inside. More military personnel loitered in the reception area. As Emily paused to look around, she felt another rifle in her back.

"Keep going!"

"Jesus Christ, I am!" Emily grunted as she carried on. They were led up several flights of stairs. More personnel filled the halls but not a single other civilian, like themselves, was in sight. Emily felt more in danger, the further she was taken. Eventually they stopped and a soldier pushed open a door.

"Get in."

The three of them stepped inside. Strangely, the room was

in good order; a few chairs were spread around but, besides heavy-duty cleaning equipment, it was exactly like a prison cell.

"Okay, I'm going to cut these restraints. If you do anything stupid one of these will shoot you. Do I make myself clear?" Emily nodded and turned to face the wall. The restraints were quickly snapped off; one by one, each of them was released. Amy and Kyle grabbed Emily.

"So now what, we wait?"

"Yes."

"For what exactly? We've been waiting almost a week for you lot to do something."

The soldiers turned and left, the last one backed out of the room, his rifle aimed at the family. The door was closed and locked. Emily dropped painfully to her knees and tightly embraced her children, letting out a cry. Her bravery seemed like stupidity now; she had put them all in danger despite being warned.

A while passed by before anyone came back. They had been left alone in the room, hearing heavy boots thudding across the carpet and the muffled voices of the soldiers. Suddenly a shadow darkened the window in the door to their room. Emily gasped as the door swung open and a soldier stepped in pointing his rifle at them. Another soldier joined the first and they stood apart aiming at the family. A third soldier also entered, his suit, though, was white and dripping liquid, Emily could only assume it was rain. The soldiers stepped back to the corners of the room. The white-suited man turned as a colleague, also dressed in white, walked into the room carrying a grey briefcase which he placed on the ground.

"Thank you, Sam. Okay, my name is Doctor Paul Young. I am

the medical lead on this operation. It's my job to run a simple blood test on you three."

"Like hell are you. I don't trust you."

"And with good reason. You're a mother, your job is to protect your children. I can only apologise for the way you were brought here, but you have to understand we are experiencing something truly terrifying ourselves."

"That doesn't give you any reason to bring us in like that."

"No, but I don't think you realise how bad things are."

"Try me, seriously."

"I can't just now. Please, I need you to do this willingly or Private Jones here will help me forcibly. Don't make me use that option."

Kyle slowly stepped forward.

"Ah brave one, aren't you? Please, I need to do this to check you aren't sick. May I?"

Kyle nodded and Doctor Young rolled up the boy's soaked sleeve and gestured to the other scientist. He placed the briefcase down and pulled a syringe kit from it, handing it to the doctor.

"Thank you. Okay, I'm going to connect a vial. I'm sure you've had an injection before, it'll be a little pinprick and I'll draw some blood. Then it'll all be done. I'll be quick."

Kyle turned his head to look at his mother, who tried to smile while her bottom lip quivered beneath her mask. Doctor Young pushed the needle into Kyle's arm: he let out a small wail as the doctor pulled on the syringe, watching carefully as the dark red liquid filled the vial.

"Ah, that's perfect, a perfect patient, thank you. What's your name?"

"K–K–Kyle."

"Good job, Kyle. Go take a seat and I'll carry on with the rest of your family okay?"

Kyle slowly wandered past his mother and sister and slumped into a seat. He rolled his sleeve down and held his arm. Emily watched as Amy stood, pulling up her sleeve and holding her arm out.

"If we're clean, do we go?"

"Let's take this a step at a time, young lady."

"It's Amy, actually," Emily called as she slowly stepped towards her daughter.

"Please don't. I need you to stay apart, just for a moment." The doctor held out his hand and Emily stopped suddenly. "Okay Amy, I take it you're the brave one here. I'll be quick so you can comfort your brother."

Amy turned away and the doctor pulled another syringe from the briefcase. Amy reacted in the same way as her brother, looking at the vial as it filled with her blood, she turned away quickly as Doctor Young pulled the needle out.

"Okay, thank you for that."

Amy rolled her sleeve down and stepped back to hold on to Kyle.

"Okay Mum–"

"It's Emily."

"Emily. Okay, Emily can you step up? I'll be brief, I promise."

She pulled her sleeve up slowly. The doctor leaned back for a moment as he stared at the cuts and bruises which covered her arm. He found himself glancing at her now he was up close, noticing that her clothes were torn, and her makeshift bandages were splitting.

"Hey, come on!"

The doctor jumped slightly and cleared his throat, "Right,

yeah." He pulled out another syringe and pushed it in to her arm. As the vial filled, he couldn't help but ask, "You've been through quite a lot then? You look like hell."

"Yeah well, it's been a rough week."

"Quite the survivor. Okay, I'm done."

"So, when will we know?"

"I'll be back. Sit tight."

The doctor placed the vials into the briefcase and closed the lid, the locks clicking quietly, "I won't make you wait long, I promise."

Both doctors walked out of the room followed by the two soldiers. The door was closed and locked once more.

Emily and her children moved restlessly from chair to chair; there wasn't much to talk about anymore. They were exhausted and drained, too tired to engage in meaningful conversation.

"Do you think we have it?" Amy asked her Mum who turned quickly.

"Amy, I think we would know by now."

"But would we? Why would they need to test us?"

"I don't know but they did, okay?"

Amy put her head in her hands and ran her fingers through to her hair, "I miss Dad."

Emily shifted uncomfortably in her chair, "Me too, Amy. Me too."

"Do you think he's. . . you know?"

"Amy don't, not now."

"But it's possible? It's been nearly a whole week and nothing!"

"Amy plea-." As she wondered what to say to comfort her daughter, loud voices split the conversation and they found themselves listening in silence to what was going on outside.

Emily wandered slowly to the door and leaned in.

"We have to get them to Castle base-"

"Doctor. I am not moving them to Castle, it's-"

"But I need to run a-"

As she leaned closer, the building shook and the power went. The emergency lights illuminated the room and the corridor in a weak and ominous green glow. Emily leaned away from the door and stepped up to her children who were slowly moving toward each other. Emily pulled them closer, and they stood frozen in place. A loud growl filled the air. The building shook again, and the roar bounced around the room once more, this time torchlight flicked along the corridor and the sound of boots on the ground moved away from them.

"Captain, report."

Emily stood, listening at the door as she squeezed her children ever tighter and desperately strained to hear what was being said on the radio. The radio request was answered with a frenzy of screams and brief gunfire, the three of them jumping as the sounds broke through.

"Captain! Shit! You two, on me," the soldier called.

Emily let go of her children, indicating to them to remain quiet. She moved slowly to the door again. Creeping towards it, she found herself stumbling back as the sounds of screaming shook her. Loud crashes and gunfire echoed round the room. A deafening shriek and the loud pounding of a hand on their door made her freeze. She covered her mouth to prevent herself from making a sound as she watched the hand leave behind a bloodied trail. Within seconds the hand was replaced by the crashing of the attacker and the door crumbled. Emily fell back and her children grabbed at her pulling her towards them. The attacker was revealed to be one of the many variations of twisted monsters. This one was long and slender like a lizard, it growled deeply as it forced its head through the door.

The three of them had nowhere to go, all they could do was watch as it battered not only the door, but the thin frame and wall with it. They huddled together screaming in fear as it lurched towards them.

"In here!" The call came from behind the monster and was followed by a barrage of gunfire, the bullets ripping into its body, its scream deafening, even in the cacophony of noise. With a crash and a whip of its tail, the monster fell, its blood oozing out and soaking into the carpet.

"Clear, on me!" the soldier's order was followed by a wall of light as the family shielded their eyes.

"Come on, get up, we have to go now!"

Emily lowered her hand a little and caught the wide-eyed reaction of the doctor who had taken their blood not so long ago, "Now! Move!"

"Guard the door! On the door now!" the doctor turned back to the soldier who nodded and ordered his comrades out of the room. "Come on you three, stay close, come on!"

Emily pulled herself to her feet and dragged her children up from the floor as they side-stepped the monster's already rotting corpse and joined the soldiers.

"Doctor, what now?" the soldier asked with panic in his voice.

"We need to get to Castle, these three are priority."

"Sir, I don't mean to be a- well maybe I do, I mean, what the hell makes them so important?"

As another soldier turned to talk to the doctor, a monster roared, and he laid a barrage of bullets into it.

"We haven't got time for this, move now!" the doctor pushed the soldier on.

"Let's move!" the soldier at the rear back-tracked behind them frantically flashing his torch from side to side as they all moved out.

The group moved with speed, stepping over each other as panic swept over them all. There was no coordination. More gunfire and screams echoed around the corridors.

The lead soldier kicked in the fire door and surveyed the stairs, "All clear!" he declared barely pausing before heading down them.

They all began to descend, Emily desperately trying to keep up as she felt her leg twinge under the strain. She knew they couldn't stop, not even for a moment. As they reached the bottom, the lead soldier paused and held his hand in the air. Everyone slowed to a complete stop. As the soldier leaned on the handle, something crashed against the door. They all moved back, flattening themselves against the wall. A monster stood in the way, roaring defiantly as bullets pierced and passed through its skin, before it dropped to the floor.

The soldier pushed down the door handle and edged his way out.

"Hold your fire, we're coming out!"

"Copy!" a terrified voice called out as they stepped out from the stairwell and met with another of the soldiers.

"Anyone else with you?" the lead soldier asked.

"Err no. They're all dead sir. It's just me."

"Stick with us we'll-"

Suddenly, the soldier dropped to the floor, face first. Torch-light piercing the darkness revealed a monster, its large tentacle arm had wrapped itself around the soldier's legs holding him firmly in its grasp.

"Help me!" the soldier screamed as he was dragged across

the floor.

The other soldiers peppered the monster with a hail of bullets as Emily and the children cowered from it. They all watched in horror as the monster's huge body tore apart to reveal a huge mouth; the poor soldier disappeared into it in a blur of blood and bone.

"Fuck! Everyone back up, back-" the lead soldier ordered the team to move away, only to find himself in the monster's grasp as it reached out again and pulled hard at his legs. The remaining soldiers turned and shot wildly at the monster.

The doctor pushed in front of the family and pointed behind them, "Move! Head for the exit sign at the end of the corridor, go!"

Emily nodded. Halfway along, she took a glance over her shoulder and saw the doctor was pulling a radio away from one of the soldiers. The doctor held the radio to his helmet, Emily couldn't hear what was being said but she had a feeling she might find out soon.

The doctor grabbed Emily and pushed her on, "Move!" He guided her to the door and pointed again.

"Kid, push the handle down!"

Amy ran to the door, swinging it open to the rain again. As they ran through it, the doctor turned back.

"Close the door! Get a car in front of it!"

The soldiers that greeted them shouted to each other and Emily watched as a large transporter slowly blocked the door.

"What's going on, what are we doing out here?" she shouted, grabbing the doctor to gain his attention, "Why are we impor-tant?" she was unfazed as rifles were pointed at her.

"You've questions, I get it but... I'm sorry," the doctor met the eyes of someone behind her, Emily twisted and found a rifle, yet again, pressed hard into her face.

Chapter 15

Doctor Young put his hands flat on the desk and looked down, breathing in and out steadily to regain his composure. The machine alongside him was whirring and building up speed. Satisfied he stepped to the side and brushed his fingers along the edge of the desk bearing his neatly arranged tools as he strode across his lab.

The doctor stopped and turned, looking at Emily as she lay unrestrained in a small cell-like room. He was close to finding something, he could tell, but only the end result would matter. He stepped up to the glass and slowly knelt down, studying her as she slept. Her body was covered in deep cuts and bruises, her clothes were heavily stained with blood, sweat and the unusual green liquid which seemed to leak from the monsters in combat and in death.

As he studied her, Emily grunted in agony as she awoke and rolled slowly on the metallic frame that was her bed. Despite her pain, she lifted herself up and frantically surveyed her surroundings, finding the doctor rising from his knees and stepping back from the glass.

"Good evening, Emily."

"Where am I?"

"You're in a secure facility, dubbed The Castle."

Emily rubbed her hand over her face and winced as she touched the large swelling covering her eye, "Did you need to hit me again?"

"Protocol dictates no one outside of this facility's personnel is to know its location. I apologise."

"Like hell you do. What am I doing in a damn glass box?"

"This is a holding cell, specifically to hold. . . you," Doctor Young held out his arms and glanced from side to side, "Maybe not for you, in particular, but for what you can give us."

"Ha, ha, okay, I've been here before and I'm telling you, I don't think it's funny."

"Emily, how long have you known?"

"Known what?" Emily stood with a grunt and pressed her bloodied hand to the glass, "What are you trying to tell me Doctor Young?"

"Emily, you're infected!"

Emily stepped back from the glass and shook her head, "No... no! If I was, I would be dead by now!"

"You have been a positive case for several days, maybe even a whole week."

"You're lying," she half-laughed, half-cried as she sidled back and slumped onto the metallic bed, "You can't be serious."

Doctor Young stepped up to the glass and folded his arms, "I'm sorry but the fact that you've survived so far puts you in an incredible position. You see, Emily, by surviving for so long you are proof the infection is not a death sentence. On the other hand, you are the cause, the one who's spreading the infection."

Emily slowly met the doctor's gaze looking for more.

"To put it bluntly, you could have been spreading it to everybody you came into contact with. Now, I ask you again, when did you realise you were infected? Please, don't play games with me, this is important. You could start convulsing at any moment and change into one of the metamorphs out there. Please, help me stop the spread."

"It started the day the town had its first attack. He changed in front of me, and I-I hit him Something covered me and... it didn't start till a day or two later when I threw up some kind of liquid."

"So, you were exposed to the purest form of the infection? Incredible!" The doctor stepped quickly to his desk and began typing on his computer.

"Doctor what does it mean? Can you cure this?"

"We're trying, I promise, but it means I cannot let you out. You are, well, the embodiment of the infection. You are the only known living human being to have been in full contact with it who's continued to live beyond the forty-eight-hour window. Well, that's almost true. . . your children-"

"What about them?" Emily jumped up. She pulled her mask off her face, peeling it away from her bloodied nose and hit the glass again, "Tell me, where they are!"

"They are alive, and they aren't infected, Emily. Whether it's genetics or luck, I don't really know, but they are infection-free."

Emily let out a huge sigh of relief and clenched her fists, "Oh, thank God for that. But what is it? What is happening? Can you at least tell me that?"

Doctor Young slowed his typing and paused for a moment, "How much do you know about the incident, the one with the space shuttle accident?"

"I know it crashed, pieces broke off and that was the reason for the lockdown, something about chemicals?"

Doctor Young shook his head and leaned back from his desk,

"No. That was the cover," the doctor sighed and brushed his hand through his hair, "Emily, the space shuttle was carrying a substance discovered on Mars. It was exposed in a bizarre incident planet-side. Long story short, they brought it back to Earth but there was an accident and the shuttle crashed. It slowly released the infection, or microbes. At first nothing happened, it was dormant. . . then, well, you know the rest."

"You mean to tell me this is an alien invasion?"

"Oh no, this isn't an invasion, it's an extermination. This thing, whatever it is, is going to wipe us out. At the moment, the infection doesn't live long but it's mutating and getting stronger as time goes on."

"You're telling me it's going to get worse?"

"The infected host turns in twenty-four to forty hours and has been known to survive a maximum of seven days. But it's changing, whatever it is, is learning, adapting to survive. Emily, if we don't figure out why you aren't dead yet, and develop a cure, the planet is only weeks away from extinction."

Emily held her head in her hands as she tried to take in this huge revelation. After all the horrendous things she'd done, everything she'd endured, she might be trapped in a glass cage as the world ended. Her children would have survived the ordeal in the Abbey for nothing. She probably wouldn't see Jack again or know his fate. Tears formed behind her eyes, her throat ached and, finally, she broke. Her strength had been completely drained from her body.

Doctor Young stepped up to the glass, "Here. I asked the soldiers to find some fresh clothes. I think it's the least I can offer you. I thought you might welcome the change."

"Thank you."

Doctor Young pulled a metal drawer out of the wall, carefully placed the clothes into the cage and pushed it closed. A green light shone, and buzzer rang into the glass cell, and Emily pulled out the garments.

"I'll give you a moment." Doctor Young smiled and pulled his ID badge from his pocket, pushing it against the screen on the wall activating another buzzer, releasing the door for him to exit.

Emily began to undress and change. The clothes provided were military fatigues and she felt strange as she pulled on the camouflage trousers and clean white vest. Deep scratches were still visible along her battered and torn chest. She ran her hands through her hair and pulled the bobble from it, the dried blood on her scalp making it difficult to free. She painfully twisted a fresh ponytail, staring at her hands as she spied the cuts on her palms.

Emily turned as the buzzer sounded and the door into the lab was pushed open. She watched as the person who had entered the room rummaged around in the lab. They clearly didn't belong as they pushed pots and equipment to the floor. As the man moved around, realisation hit her. Meeting his eyes, she was almost overcome with emotion and she let out a cry.

"Jack?"

Chapter 16

"Emily?" Jack darted to the glass, putting his hand up to it. Emily moved her own hand across the window and placed it parallel to her husband's.

"Oh my God, Jack, how the hell did you find me?"

"Alan told me you were taken."

"Jesus, how did you even get in here?"

"Honestly, I don't know," Jack laughed awkwardly, "I can't believe I've found you."

"Where were you?"

Emily and Jack both jumped back from the glass as Doctor Young buzzed himself back into the lab. The doctor stood, horrified, as he reached for a medical knife from the table and held it out, "What are you doing in here? Who are you?"

"I want to know why my wife is in this fucking glass box!"

"Your wife? Sir-" Doctor Young stepped to the side as Jack lurched forward holding his own knife, "Okay, woah, now hang on-"

"No! Answer my question! Why is she locked up in a glass box?"

"I don't think you-" the doctor jumped as Jack slammed his free fist against the table and held the knife towards him.

"Answer me now! I have been without my family for too long. You will answer my question! Now!"

"She's infected," Doctor Young told.

Tears welled up in Jack's eyes again as he turned to his wife, "You're lying."

"I wish I was," the doctor went to his computer and spun the monitor around. The text on the screen simply read 'Positive', "but there is no doubt."

"No. . ." Jack slowly stepped up to the glass and put his arm above him to rest his head, "I've been without you for what feels like forever. This can't be how it ends."

"Jack I-" Emily stuttered as she tried to speak as they both began to come to terms with the dark truth to their reunion, "I'm sorry, I should have-"

"No, no, Emily. It's not your fault, I should have found you sooner! I got stuck in the damn shelter, I couldn't get out, it locked me in. I'm such an idiot. . ."

"No Jack-"

"I should have tried harder. For you. For the kids," Jack turned to face the doctor, "Where are my children?"

"They're safe-"

"Where are they?"

"They're in a holding area. They are safe, I promise you. Unlike your wife, they're not infected," the doctor began to reach for something under the desk as Jack watched, "I'll let you go free, just leave now. If the military find you, they will execute you, I-"

"I'm taking her with me," Jack rubbed his eyes and cleared his throat, "I'm taking my wife from here."

"Absolutely not, are you crazy?"

"Open the box!"

"Jack-" Emily shook her head, "Jack, I'm sick. I can't-"

"No, I won't... I can't go without you."

"Jack, I understand but-"

"No! No! You don't understand what I'm feeling at all! Don't tell me you understand! Don't tell me you understand how it feels to be apart from your family, not knowing what's going on in the world, screaming in the concrete tomb you locked yourself in, hoping, praying you'll see them again. Then when you do, you can't even hold them," Jack turned and glanced up at the red handle tucked in the wall, "Emily we're going home."

"Jack no!" Emily stood in the middle of the glass box as the door hissed and released.

"Jack stop now!" Doctor Young stepped up to Jack, a mask pulled over his mouth and a pistol in his hand, "Your wife cannot leave. If she goes, she will kill you."

Emily glanced at the open door and back to the feuding men, deciding to make a run for it.

"Emily, no wait-" Doctor Young turned to point his gun at her before lowering his weapon. Jack stepped towards his wife with his hands in the air, his face twisted in confusion. Emily stood shaking, holding the medical knife to her own throat.

"Jack. . . please. You have to go without me."

Jack took in the situation for a moment before voices from behind the door interrupted them. Doctor Young moved with speed and smashed the bottom of his pistol into the panel which sparked and puffed briefly.

"Jack, you have thirty seconds to leave before they get into this room and shoot you." The doctor watched as Jack's gaze never left his wife, "Jack you can save your children."

Jack dropped the knife as the doctor handed him a set of keys. Turning them in his hand, he noticed the car emblem branded into the black fob.

"It's for a silver Mercedes. Push the button to find it. Your children are in the holding bay. Follow the signs. Survive. For her!"

Jack stood in disbelief, his head pounding with the weight of the decision he was about to make.

"Jack," Emily lowered the knife as she sobbed, "Save our children."

Just then, the soldiers breached the door and Jack ducked in surprise, fumbling for the door to his right.

"Intruder!" the lead soldier shouted before firing an opening shot. The other soldiers followed, their bullets tearing up the walls around Jack as he fell out into the corridor and made a break for it.

Jack stumbled as he pushed his way through the staff who screamed as the gunfire echoed down the corridor, and they melted into the walls to get out of the way. In the chaos, Jack tumbled into a woman in a white coat; she screamed, pushing him away as he pulled the lanyard from around her neck. Slamming the lanyard into the panel Jack fell into the holding area.

"Dad!" Jack turned as the door closed. His smile was wide as Amy and Kyle rose from a pair of metal chairs to embrace him.

"Dad, you're alive!"

"I'm alive! Oh my God, you guys." Jack squeezed his children tightly. He had waited for what felt like a lifetime for this moment and he was going to make the most of it. The three of them pulled away from each other, Jack wiped away a tear as Amy peered over his shoulder.

"Dad, where's Mum?" Before Jack could answer her question, the door by which he had entered was being battered once again.

"We can talk later. Right now, we need to get out of here." Jack jumped up and looked around, trying to spot a way out, "Okay behind you, get through those doors, go!"

The three of them sprinted through the doorway. The door behind them splintered as the soldiers charged into the room. They opened fire as the family entered into the large room. Jack pulled his children to the floor, taking cover behind a large metal container. The room was vast. In the centre stood some incredibly tall pieces of black panelling from a submarine, the pieces laid out like a jigsaw. The room was littered with parts for its construction. Jack leaned back, the soldiers were bracing the wall and preparing to move for them.

"Okay you two, we have to run and we can't stop. Use the big containers to protect you. These soldiers will hurt us. Run. . . now!"

Jack lifted Amy and urged her on, then turning to Kyle and pushing him on behind her. Each of the three moved at a different pace. They were completely vulnerable to the soldiers, who fired at them without hesitation.

As he moved, Jack glanced from side to side, trying to spot where the soldiers were. They seemed to have about five seconds' advantage. He saw a group of soldiers high above them on a gantry; the long barrel of a sniper's rifle was pointing directly towards the family.

"Amy, stop!" Jack grabbed Kyle around his waist and reached for Amy to pull her back.

The sniper's bullet ricocheted off the scaffolding, allowing the family a second to stop and avoid disaster. Amy's eyes were wide as she stared directly ahead of her in shock. She brought her hands up in front of her and twisted them for her Dad to see. Jack twitched as another bullet clinked off the metal frame and he found himself looking at his daughter who sat bleeding on the floor.

"It's going to be okay Amy, we're nearly out. Just one more run okay?"

Amy burst into tears as she gently squeezed her bleeding palms.

"Please Amy, you're nearly there. We're nearly-"

Hearing a fracas, the three of them ducked and Jack peered around the metal frame to see what was going on. Looking up, the snipers on the gantry were now caught up in a fight for their own survival. A large monster had breached the door behind them and had taken but a moment to batter the soldiers who screamed in fear.

Jack seized this opportunity to escape with his children and turned back to them, "Okay. Once more, okay. One metal box at a time." Amy and Kyle trembled but nodded their heads. "Now!" Jack pulled them both back to their feet and pushed them forward, moving them between the metal containers, scaffolding and crane legs. Using any cover they could find, they managed to reach the door and finally escape.

Jack pushed on the handle but found himself wrapped in the tight grip of a vine. The children stumbled and screamed as the monster moved, enraged as it bled violently from its torso. The monster's blood streamed towards Jack who pulled away hard to avoid suffering the same fate as his wife. Slowly the monster pulled on Jack's arm as his children desperately tried to free him. They screamed as they pulled once last time. Jack found himself almost flattening his children as the monster suddenly released its deathly grip. A barrage of bullets had put the monster onto its back. Jack turned to face the soldiers who had finished it off. He stood arms wide and completely defenceless as they turned their rifles on him and his children.

Before he could beg for their lives, one of the large cranes, that had been used to hoist machinery, crumbled under the weight of the monster which had smashed through the glass panel in the roof. Many soldiers were crushed beneath it.

One surviving soldier urged, "Damn it, move! Get out of here!" He waved to Jack and began to fire at the monster.

Jack hesitated for a moment.

"Go!"

Jack turned on his heel and pushed the bar, releasing the fire door. The three of them tumbled out into the rainstorm and away from the chaos of the base which was rapidly being overrun.

Chapter 17

Jack paused for a moment as he surveyed the chaos. The base had been the most heavily defended building in the town and, in an instant, it had become completely overrun, nobody was safe. As the door swung closed, the soldier who had got them out ran to them. Jack shielded his children again, but the soldier raised his hands.

"Listen. . . I'm not going to hurt you," the soldier turned to the base and pointed, "This is what I was protecting and, well, I guess that's pointless now. Anyway, you have to get out of here." He looked down as Jack produced a car key, "You want the cars, they're right here. Take one and go. You're going to have about ninety seconds before this place is levelled."

"What do you mean?"

The soldier pulled his radio from his kevlar vest and shook it, "In the event of the base being compromised we're ordered to call in an airstrike," the soldier pointed to the sky, "Up there is a very large gunship, mate. I would move now."

Jack hesitated as he watched the soldier pull his heavy bio-hazard mask from his head and breathe in deeply.

The soldier put his radio to his mouth, "This is Romeo Nine of Castle base requesting an extermination."

The radio crackled momentarily, and Jack stumbled back and prepared to run.

"Copy that Romeo Nine, requesting authorisation code."

"Guys go, now!" The soldier lunged forward and ushered Jack on. Jack turned and clicked the key fob looking for the brief flash of the car headlights. As he spotted them he pumped the air.

"Alright you two, get in that car!" Jack followed his children through the tangle of battered cars that surrounded them and breathed a sigh of relief as he found the car he held the key to was almost unscathed. The children pulled the car doors open and flung themselves in, slamming them behind them. Jack settled himself into the car and fumbled to push the key into the ignition. As he twisted it, the engine roared to life.

"Belts on!"

The children quickly pulled their seatbelts into position. The bag he was carrying, dug sharply into Jack's back. He dropped the handbrake and floored the accelerator. The car lurched forward, and Jack began the task of darting between the debris and the fighting that surrounded the base. He made little effort to avoid scratching the clearly expensive car, he was only concentrating on their survival.

"Dad, where's Mum?" Amy leaned forward and hung onto her father's car seat, "You said she was going to meet us."

"Amy please, not now."

"No! Right now! Where is Mum?"

"Amy, I said not now!" Jack pressed the brakes and turned the steering wheel aggressively as they exited the base, "Please-"

"Dad, why isn't Mum here?" Kyle joined in the questioning and began to sob, "Where's Mum?"

"Guys your-"

The conversation was cut short as Jack caught sight of the events unfolding behind them. As he watched through his mirrors, the base twisted and exploded into a huge fireball. In the sky the gunship was firing without mercy, leaving nothing standing.

Amy swung round and began to scream, pulling on Jack's seat, "Dad, why did you leave her in there?"

"I had no choice-"

"Yes, you did Mum was- watch out!"

Jack flicked his eyes forward, and twisted the wheel violently, to avoid the monster which stood proudly blocking the way. As the car slid across the bridge, it barely missed the creature which left a glancing blow on its side for good measure.

Gripping the steering wheel harder Jack bit his lip and tried to think of how he was going to break the harrowing news to his children.

"Guys, your Mum was sick."

"Mum was sick, but she wasn't a monster. . ." Kyle slumped back in his chair and turned to look out of the window.

As Jack tried both to spot the road and glance at his son, a short burst of bullets ricocheted off the car's side door. Looking in his wing mirror, moments before the next burst tore it off, Jack spied a group of military jeeps following them off the bridge, along the road through the Town Hall's eerily deserted outdoor camp.

Jack grunted as pressed the accelerator and sped through the camp's torn tents and the equipment littering the floor.

"Kids stay down!"

More bullets bounced off the car as the children quickly ducked and held each other. Jack leaned forward as far as he could to stay low whilst still driving the car, weaving it through the abandoned vehicles that blocked their path. A short time later, Jack turned at the library. Amy looked up momentarily and was reminded of their brief ordeal. She held her brother even tighter in the back of the car.

As they tried to get away, the soldiers were gaining, and bodywork continued to fall from their damaged vehicle. Despite its power, the dragging rear bumper was making the escape harder and Jack had no answer to the bullets that were peppering the car. The children screamed at each barrage of bullets or whenever something battered their vehicle.

"We're nearly there. . ."

"Where are we going?" Amy lifted her head, jumping as the rear window broke and showered them in glass.

"Just hang on please. . ." Jack gripped the steering wheel as he turned the corner and spied the military checkpoint he had been referred to earlier. He twisted and tried to pull his backpack to his chest, but he found he had to keep his hands on the wheel as the road became almost undriveable.

"Amy, open my backpack!"

Amy released her brother, curling up in her seat as another bullet flicked off the car.

"Please Amy, get the radio!"

Amy leaned forward and unzipped the backpack, sobbing as she flailed around, pushing aside whatever was inside. She paused as she wrapped her hands around the radio and forced it out of the large pocket.

"Thank you!" Jack took the radio into one of his hands, gripping the steering wheel harder with the other, "Okay' I'm here. You need to do it now!"

Jack released the radio and glanced back.

"Okay one last time. Stay down whatever happens, okay?"

As his children stared at each other in fear, Jack shifted the car up a gear and held the steering wheel as they snaked over the brow of the hill.

"Dad what are-"

"Shh! Stay down!" Jack flailed his arm behind him and looked to his left, trying to catch a glimpse of some welcoming lights, "Come on, please. . ." Jack kept his foot on the accelerator for a moment longer before he lifted it slightly, "Shit. . . no!" He hit the steering wheel just as the radio buzzed to life.

"Jack- Keep going-"

He turned again and a large set of headlights lit up the opposing hill.

"Yes! Hold on kids!"

Jack accelerated one last time and the three of them screamed as they raced for the checkpoint. Bullets bounced off every inch of the car, then came a heavy booming noise and the inside of the car flickered a bright orange as it was slammed into spin after spin. It finally came to rest when it met with something strong enough to halt the momentum it had gained.

All three coughed heavily. Jack elbowed and kicked the door open, falling out onto the rain-soaked road which cooled his friction-burned hands. He painfully hopped around the car, noticing its battered exterior. He pulled hard on the passenger door and leaned inside, releasing the seatbelts holding his children.

"Come on kids, it's nearly over, one more move."

Jack helped his children out of the car. They stared at the devastation in front of them. Amy paused for a moment and wondered just what her Dad had done. Jack drew his children off the road and painfully pushed open a wooden gate. The children stood and watched as Jack pulled a dark green sheet away to reveal another car. Jack stumbled forward and untaped the car key from the back of the wing mirror and clicked the electronic lock releasing the doors.

"In. Now!" The children jumped in and Jack wasted no time in starting up the new car and hitting the accelerator hard, the wooden boards beneath its wheels just giving the car enough traction to enable the getaway it was being asked to provide.

Jack swung the car around the corner and didn't look back. The children stared at the checkpoint as it burned, lighting up the jet-black sky as the rain continued to fall. Jack breathed a sigh of relief and let out a small whimper. Checking the wing mirror, he smiled and reached his hand behind him allowing his children to hold it. Finally, it was over. He had found his family and saved them. Nearly.

Chapter 18

Dear Emily. We did it. You, did it. You got our children to safety. You passed the baton, and I reached the finish line. I guess this isn't quite the end, for us anyway. Me and the kids left a little memorial across the way from the pier on Lake Windermere, our spot. I love you.

Jack closed the rain-soaked, blood-stained diary and placed the palms of his hands on it one last time. He detected the faint aroma of his wife's perfume and clenched his fists tightly. Jack still felt guilty for not having been there for the children and Emily, but, having had the chance to read through her small diary of events, he knew that, in time, he would be able to forgive himself. Jack smiled as Kyle shuffled under his arm and patted the diary.

"What are you doing with Mum's diary?"

"Just writing one more thing in there before we leave it behind."

"Why?" Kyle looked up to his father who just smiled and got to his feet.

"Just something I have to do, son"

Jack sank to his knees and placed the diary snug against the small cross that he had constructed out of nearby sticks. He sat there for a moment and desperately tried to hold it together, tears steadily building while he took it all in. Amy and Kyle slipped under his arms and they sat there together to share in their final goodbye. Jack wondered how the children felt but couldn't bring himself to utter a word, fearing his own voice would crack with emotion.

Jack stood, using his sleeve to wipe away his tears, and cleared his throat.

"Okay kids, go pack up the stuff. We can head off in a minute."

The children nodded and he watched them run off. Amy lightly pushed her brother as the pair of them playfully headed off to the small camp they had set up in the cover of the forest. Jack turned back to the lake and scrutinised the pier. His smile faded as he surveyed the scene, watching as the monsters lingered along its once busy slipway. In the middle of the lake one of the boats, which once ran laps for tourists, stood almost like the Titanic with its nose poking above the water. Jack dared not think about what could be lying in wait for them or be in the water. Could the monsters swim? He shook his head, he just had to worry about his family and their next step, whatever that maybe.

Jack turned and headed back for his children.

"Hey, come on you two, I said pack up. Time to go, okay?" He stepped up to Kyle and ruffled his hair, "Come on, you're not going to let your sister win the last chocolate, are you?"

The children laughed and rushed to cram everything into their bags. Jack laughed and began to pack his own gear, his clean backpack, which they had taken from a nearby shop, was neatly arranged with fresh survival items. He stood and pulled the car key from his pocket clicking the button to release the boot lock.

"Right go on, times up!"

The children hurried and zipped up their bags, throwing them into the boot and pulling frantically on the car doors, racing each other as they clambered in. Jack laughed as he listened to them argue about who got into the car first and who was the slowest. It was a pleasant sound, the sound of innocent enjoyment. He zipped up his own bag and hauled it over his back, walking to the car something rustled in the treeline out of his sight. Jack stopped and quickly looked from side to side. Nothing. Jack threw his bag into the boot, shutting it with a satisfying clunking sound and climbing into his car.

"Okay you two. Are you ready?"

"Where are we going, Dad?"

Jack paused for a moment as he glanced at the dwindling fuel gauge and sighed.

"Somewhere safe."

Jack clicked the car key forward and the engine purred to life. As he dropped the handbrake and steadily drove down the country road, Amy reached forward and pulled a notebook from the seat pocket. She pulled the stylish pen from the binding and clicked the top. Placing pen to paper, with a smile on her face, she began to write –

Dear Diary. . .

About the Author

Chris Pease is a Cumbrian writer. When he isn't plotting some end of the world story, he can be found in the seat of a go kart, raising a small family of nerds or the usual day job.

Also by Chris Pease

The Prepper

Lakeland Ranger, Matt Richards, lives on Lake Windermere. Struggling with his own personal circumstances, an unknown threat is lurking out in the open and threatens to change the troubled Ranger for good.

When he finds himself at a crossroad, Matt summons the courage to ask for help and finds himself thrown in to a world in disarray. Will it be too late for the troubled Ranger?

Available exclusively at www.chrispeaseauthor.com